THE CHRISTMAS REBOUND

A HOLIDAY NOVELLA

CALI MELLE

Copyright © 2024 by Cali Melle

All rights reserved.

No part of this book may be reproduced in any form or by any electronic or mechanical means, including information storage and retrieval systems, without written permission from the author, except for the use of brief quotations in a book review.

This book is a work of fiction and any resemblance to any person, living or dead, or any events or occurrences is purely coincidental. The characters and story lines are created purely by the author's imagination and are used fictitiously.

No A.I. has been used in the production of this fictitious work.

Edited by Rumi Khan

Proofread by Alexandra Cowell

I see you've made the naughty list again…

CHAPTER ONE
QUINN

"Why are there marshmallows in the fish tank?"

My eyebrows pull together as I hear the words behind me. I turn around slowly, my feet pivoting on the tile floor in Lincoln and Nova's kitchen as I look in the direction of where his voice came. Through the mingling people, I see him and lift my mug to my lips to conceal my grin as I see Hayes Wilder crouched down in front of Nova's daughter.

They're tucked away in the corner of the kitchen where no one saw what was going on. Hayes smiles at her while holding the soggy marshmallow in his hand as they stand next to the small tank on the table along the wall. His lips move as he says something else to her and she takes off running into the living room. Hayes stands upright and shakes his head as he walks toward me, stopping to throw the piece of food into the trash can.

"Kids," he says with a soft chuckle as he walks over to where I'm standing by the counter. "I don't know what gave her the idea that her little fish can eat marshmallows."

I laugh too, shaking my head as my eyes focus solely on him. "Thank God you were there to save the day."

Hayes folds his arm across his torso and gives a bow. "I'm just here to serve, Miss Sanders."

I half choke on a breath of air as his words slide across my eardrums in a sultry tone. Hayes doesn't comment on my coughing fit and instead raises an eyebrow as he reaches past me to fill his glass with the alcoholic Christmas concoction Lincoln made. The faint smell of Hayes's cologne infiltrates my senses and I resist the urge to push him away from me.

I should have known better than to come to a holiday party thrown by one of the players from the team I work for. Working in a male-dominated field, I've almost become one of the guys in their eyes, so when Lincoln and Nash both mentioned the party during one of their therapy sessions, it wasn't abnormal. I did try to turn down the offer, but after they got Hayes to bother me about it, it was hard to say no.

It's not like a boundary was being crossed. My friendships with the guys are all strictly platonic. Working in close quarters with a bunch of male athletes requires having lines drawn from the start. Thankfully, I haven't run into any issues with any of the players on the team. I'm the assistant physical therapist so we do a lot of hands-on work with them.

Although there are boundaries, that doesn't mean I'm blind or fully immune to some of their charm... mainly Hayes Wilder, if I'm being honest. He plays right wing for the Aston Archers and has been coming to see me more often than needed lately.

The tension in the air between us has been palpable, but I've been doing my best to ignore it. It's in everyone's best interest if we all remain professional, but I've noticed a few things that have me questioning what he's up to.

Especially the comment he just made to me.

"What are your plans for the holiday, Doc?"

I take a sip of my drink and let out a sigh. "Well, my family lives out of state so I'm supposed to go have lunch at Luke's grandmother's tomorrow."

Hayes curls his upper lip in distaste. "Luke," he sneers at my boyfriend's name, like the thought alone is enough to prick his skin. "You're still keeping that guy around?"

"Luke's a good guy," I argue, my eyebrows pulling together. Luke and I have been dating on and off for the past year, but he's been a little distant lately, so I'm not sure if I'm trying to convince myself or Hayes here.

My work schedule is pretty insane and he's been complaining about it for a while. Luke has also made it clear that he doesn't like me working with a bunch of men. I would be lying if I said the comments he made didn't piss me off, but I've been doing my best to ignore them.

"That's debatable, Quinn," Hayes says with irritation in his tone. Gone is the playfulness and instead he's giving me a stern look. "I told you before, I don't get a good vibe from the guy."

"You met him one time. I hardly think that's long enough to make a judgment on someone."

He shakes his head as his eyes burn holes into mine. "Have you forgotten everything you told me about him?"

My mouth is instantly dry and it's a struggle to try and swallow. The memory is fresh in my brain, regardless of how many times I've tried to extinguish it. One night after work, I went out to get a drink after fighting with Luke the night before. I ended up running into Hayes and after a few drinks, I told him things I shouldn't have said.

Mainly about our sex life... or lack thereof.

Luke has never been a sexual person and I've tried to adjust my own expectations with that, but it's been hard. I crave the connection and honestly, I just enjoy the pleasure. He's made me feel weird in the past, like there's something wrong with me for having a more intense sex drive than he has.

Hayes suggested that night that maybe there's someone else and there are times where I catch myself wondering the same thing.

"No, I didn't forget," I tell him, my voice low enough that no one can hear. "I wish both of us could forget I mentioned any of that."

"Well, that's unfortunate." He lets out a soft chuckle before clicking his tongue. "Lucky for both of us, that's something I'm not bound to forget." He leans toward me again, reaching for a napkin that he doesn't need as his face brushes the side of mine. "One day when you find yourself single, I'd love to show you what it's actually supposed to be like."

My breath catches in my throat. "Like what is?"

I instantly regret speaking the words without any thought behind it, but there's a burning curiosity within me. I'm dying to know, to hear, what it is he would do.

"What it's like when someone cares about your pleasure and wants to take care of you."

He slowly pulls away and my heart hammers in my chest as I find myself staring him head on. "Don't be foolish, Hayes. We both know you're a smooth talker, so don't think I'm going to just fall for your words like that."

He tilts his head to the side, raising an eyebrow at me. "You don't think I mean it?"

"I think you probably say a lot of things to women to make them feel better about themselves."

He straightens his head, his eyes not leaving mine. "If you felt my cock right now, I think you'd know these aren't just words."

Holy shit.

"Tell me, Doc," he says softly as people move around us, no one seeming to notice either of us standing in the kitchen together. "We've been tiptoeing around each other for long enough. I think it's time we explore whatever this is between us."

Breaking away from his gaze, I quickly glance around the room, feeling the blush already spreading across my face. I make sure no one is looking and quickly grab his hand, pulling him with me as I duck out of the kitchen and into a room off to the side. I don't know what room I was imagining it would be, but I didn't think it would be the damn laundry room.

Releasing his hand, I spin on my heel as the door closes behind us. As I turn around to face him, I practically collide with his chest as he moves toward me. "I didn't mean right now, but if that's what you want, I don't think I possess the ability to tell you no."

"You know we can't, Hayes." My voice is stern, yet I don't feel the same strength inside. He's in my space, his hands on my hips as he backs me toward the washer. I don't protest as he lifts me up with ease and gently sets me down on it.

"We can't or you don't want to?"

Somehow my hands end up on his shoulders. "I never said that."

A smirk pulls on the corner of his lips. He slowly begins to trail his hands up my torso, reaching for the sides of my cardigan. His fingertips are soft and light as he begins to push it away from my shoulders, exposing my skin. My heart pounds erratically in my chest, my stomach performing an acrobatic routine as he slides his fingers under the straps of my tank top.

"Do you know how long I've waited to touch you?" he murmurs, his face inching closer to me. "All these months of physical therapy sessions with you have been pure torture."

"I think I might have an idea," I admit as a rush of warmth spreads through my body. "You're not alone in feeling that way.."

He tilts his head to the side, his lips lightly brushing mine as my eyelids flutter closed. I'm expecting his kiss, but instead, he pulls back the slightest bit. "We shouldn't do this, should we?"

"I mean if someone finds out, it probably won't end well," I remind him as the thought of the different policies and agreements I had to sign when I accepted my job for the team crosses my mind.

"The last thing either of us need is to get caught."

My eyes drop down to his lips, watching as his tongue darts out to wet them. "Right. They have policies against this kind of behavior."

"Hmm," he murmurs again, his breath fanning across my face. "Perhaps we both deserve some kind of punishment for our actions."

The warmth is building in the pit of my stomach as his hands slide along my collarbone and begin to make their way up the sides of my neck. I spread my knees apart, letting him in as he steps between my legs. "You would never break the rules, would you?"

"Oh, no." He lets out a soft chuckle as he slides one hand behind my head, pushing through my hair as he grips the nape of my neck. "I'm a good boy. I don't do bad things like that."

"Never," I practically moan as his face lowers back to mine again. He pauses, his big brown eyes bouncing back and forth between mine as time is suspended between us.

"Fuck the policies, Doc."

His lips find mine in a rush as his fingers dig into the flesh on the back of my neck. He tastes like bourbon and gingerbread. My hands grip his shoulders, my legs instinctively wrapping around his waist as he kisses me with an intensity that rocks me to my core. He steals the air from my lungs, consuming me, breathing me in as his mouth melts to mine.

I kiss him back, lost in the moment as all our inhibitions fade away. His tongue slides along the seam of my mouth and I part my lips, letting him deepen the kiss. He kisses me like I've never been kissed before. There's urgency, yet tenderness. Need and lust building and mixing together.

We're not in Lincoln's laundry room. We're not at this stupid Christmas party. And I don't have to go to a fucking holiday lunch tomorrow with my boyfriend. My boyfriend who has never kissed me like this before.

Fuck.

What am I doing right now?

There's a sudden knocking on the door that

manages to thrust us back into reality. My body goes rigid, and Hayes groans against my lips before pulling away abruptly. I move away from him, my legs falling from his waist as I give him a gentle push.

"Fuck, Hayes. Someone is at the door."

"Goddammit." He lets out a frustrated breath before running a hand through his light brown hair. "Who could possibly need this room right now?"

Whoever it is knocks a little harder with a little more urgency. "Wilder. I know you're in there. Open the door."

"Jesus Christ." He glances at me as I hop off the washer, hastily attempting to make myself look a little less disheveled, like I wasn't just making out with him in the damn laundry room. "Are you good?"

I let out a harsh, half-hopeless laugh. "I mean, I think whoever is on the other side is going to know we weren't in here rehearsing fucking Christmas carols together."

"Maybe not." Hayes smirks with mischief dancing in his eyes and I want to slap the look off his face. "But I would love to make you sing."

I narrow my eyes at him, crossing my arms over my chest. "You're not helping right now."

He purses his lips, quickly glancing around the

room before his eyes stop behind me. "Do you think you can fit in there?"

My eyebrows pull together as I slowly turn around to see what he's pointing at. I pause for a second, staring at the cabinet. "Maybe."

"Honestly, I don't care if anyone sees us together, but if you don't want anyone to know, this is probably your only option."

This is absolutely ridiculous. I don't know what the hell I'm thinking—or if I'm even thinking at all. There's another knock on the door and the knob jiggles as I drop down onto my knees and open the cabinet door. There are only a few things inside and I manage to push them to the side before I climb in. My knees are in my face and Hayes stifles a laugh as I give him the middle finger.

He blows me a kiss, shuts the cabinet door, and conceals me in the darkness before he opens the door to the laundry room. "Hey," I hear him say to whoever is on the other side.

"What the hell were you doing in here with the door locked?" Carson Ford's voice fills the laundry room. "You're in here alone?"

"Yeah, I was on the phone and it was quiet in here," Hayes lies to him. "What do you need?"

"Nova was looking for you because she's handing out gifts she got for the team."

I strain to hear, listening as the two of them leave, then I hear the door shutting behind them. It feels like an eternity as I wait a solid minute before climbing from the cramped space. I fix the things in the cabinet and straighten my clothes before reaching for the door. No one sees me as I slip out of the laundry room and grab my things.

I make a hasty exit from the house, heading out through the back door as I quietly make my way out to the street where my car is parked. As I stop by the side of it and glance back at the house, I see Hayes standing by the window.

The corners of his lips lift and he winks.

A ragged breath escapes me as I climb into my car and quickly pull away from the curb. I can still smell Hayes's cologne and the memory of his lips against mine is still so fresh. Fuck me for wishing we wouldn't have been interrupted.

Merry Christmas Eve.

CHAPTER TWO
QUINN

Standing at the front door, I adjust my weight on my feet, feeling the cold air wrapping around me as I juggle the pie in my hand and knock on the wooden surface. I texted Luke earlier this morning to see if he wanted to drive together, but he didn't answer. We talked about lunch here last week and he gave me the address, so I came here at the time we discussed.

The door slowly opens and a middle-aged woman stands on the other side. A bright smile drifts across her lips as she takes in my appearance. "Hi. Merry Christmas!"

"Merry Christmas to you too!"

"May I help you with something?"

My eyebrows pull together. "Is Luke here?"

A strange look passes across her face and she rolls her lips between her teeth and nods. "Yes…" Her voice trails off into an awkward pause before she speaks again. "Let me get him."

My spine stiffens and I push my shoulders back as I plaster on a fake smile and nod. She doesn't invite me in and simply closes the door as she disappears back into the house. Dread builds in the pit of my stomach. Nothing about this feels right and I resist the urge to turn around and leave.

The door opens up again, and Luke abruptly steps out onto the porch, invading my space. I take an uncomfortable step backward. "Hey," he says in a rush, glancing over his shoulder at the house as he closes the door. "What are you doing here?"

I glance through the crack, seeing another woman standing in the foyer watching him closing the door. That's the moment I know the truth. The truth I've been suspecting this entire time.

"Who did you tell her I am?"

Luke stares at me, the color draining from his face. "She knows who you are," he admits, his voice low and filled with regret.

"So, you invited both of us to lunch at your grandmother's on purpose?"

"No, I didn't think you'd be able to come," he

says, shaking his head. "It's not what it looks like, Quinn."

"I think it is exactly what it looks like," I argue, my tone sharp and jagged. "Who is she and how long has this been going on?"

His throat bobs as he swallows hard. "She works at the firm," he tells me, and I can't tell if he actually feels regretful or if it's a facade. "It hasn't been going on long. Her family doesn't live locally so I invited her to come here today."

I can't help myself as I let out a harsh laugh. "This is something else, Luke. Really." I stop and shake my head. "This is over. We're done."

"I'm sorry, Quinn," he says quietly, shifting his weight awkwardly. "You know things haven't been good between us for a while and I didn't mean for you to find out this way."

"Please, just fucking save it," I snap at him as I blow out a breath through my nose. "Here's your fucking pie, you piece of shit."

I go to hand it to him, but as he reaches for it, I drop it onto the porch. It's childish, but fuck him. The glass breaks the instant it hits the surface beneath us and liquids from the pie splash up onto his perfectly pressed khaki pants.

"What the fuck, Quinn?"

"Oh, I'm sorry, did I get something on your pants?" I ask him, feeling the anger build up inside me. I'm not usually one who lets things get to me, but this is something entirely different. Not only has he been deceiving me, but now he's made me look like a complete idiot.

I look back at him, smiling before staring at his mouth "I think you got something on your face too."

Luke parts his lips as he goes to say something, but I silence him with my fist as I punch him directly in the mouth. The ring on my finger splits open his lip and blood rushes across his bright white teeth. He's fucking pissed and his eyebrows scrunch together as he lifts his hand to his mouth. "Are you fucking kidding me?"

"Oops, I think I made it worse," I say, shrugging with the sweetest smile. "Happy holidays, you fucking piece of shit."

Without another word, I spin on my heel and head away from the house, quickly walking back to my car. Adrenaline courses through my body and I can't even feel the throbbing in my hand as I quickly pull away from his grandmother's house. My stomach is in knots and I can't help but laugh to keep myself from crying as I head back to my place.

I'm sure I look like a damn psychopath, but who the hell cares?

I stare down at the growing bruise across my knuckles. I underestimated my own strength and how hard his teeth were when I punched my ex in the face. It's not something I've ever done before or something I'm even proud of, but fuck it.

I feel like my actions are justifiable and that's all that matters right now.

The bartender turns around to face me, his eyes dropping down to my hand before looking back up at me as I take my third martini from him. "Looks like you've got a story there."

"I promise it's not an exciting one," I tell him with a half laugh. "My boyfriend—well, ex—accidentally invited me and the other woman he's been seeing to his family Christmas dinner."

He makes a face. "That completely explains the bruises. I'm sure he deserved much worse than that."

"It is what it is," I say, lifting my glass into the air. "To the happiest of holidays, right?"

He grabs a water from behind the bar and lifts it to cheers me. "To the shitty holidays opening up new doors for you."

We both drink to that and he offers me a soft smile before heading over to help the other few loners that are here. It was one of the only bars I could find open today, and the last thing I was going to do was stay at home nursing a stupid broken heart.

I don't even know that my heart is broken. My pride took a hit I wasn't expecting.

Thinking back on our relationship, Luke wasn't that great. He wasn't a terrible boyfriend, but he wasn't a good partner. He was very selfish and self-serving. Most things we did together were what he wanted to do. It wasn't often that he asked me what I wanted.

Especially in the bedroom.

That was where our relationship severely lacked. He made it seem like a chore, like he didn't even want anything between us. I don't know why I let it go on for as long as I did. I don't know why I stayed or put up with any of his shit. There was a part of me that thought maybe it was me—like I was the one who had something wrong with them.

"If you felt my cock right now, I think you'd know these aren't just words."

I instantly blush at the memory of the words Hayes spoke to me last night. I couldn't help but feel guilty for kissing him, but after finding out what Luke has been up to, I feel no regret now. If anything, I wish I had a chance to do it over again.

A chance for him to show me how differently things can be with someone else.

I'm sure the moment has passed now, but one last Christmas wish won't hurt…

CHAPTER THREE
CHASE

As I adjust my shirt, I turn back and watch Hayes as he slides his feet into his sneakers. He slowly stands upright, his gaze meeting mine.

"What's wrong?" he asks, a touch of concern washing over his expression. "Do you not feel like going out tonight?"

I stare at him for a moment, narrowing my eyes slightly as I remember the last time I decided to go out with him. "That depends on if you're going to try to set me up with someone again."

Hayes half rolls his eyes as he grabs his cap, pushes his light brown hair away from his forehead, and puts it on. "Nope, that won't be happening again. You're on your own now."

"I mean, in all fairness, I never did ask for your

help," I remind him as we both head out of our condo and walk through the building.

"No, you didn't." Hayes pauses as he holds the door open for me. We fall back into step with one another as we walk to the street where the car is waiting for us. "I think we just need to find someone who fits both of us."

Abruptly coming to a halt, I whip my head to the side to look at him as he reaches for the door. "What?"

Hayes glances at me and shrugs. This isn't the first time we've had a talk like this, but it's the first time he's the one suggesting it. "I've been thinking about what you said that night and I think you're right. We may not work out with just the two of us, but who's to say it wouldn't work if we had a third?"

I let his words seep into my brain, creeping into the crevices of my mind. Hayes and I have had an attraction to one another for years. We've acted on it before, but neither of us wanted to give up women to exclusively be together. We've shared before, but finding someone who fit us both was a weird balance.

We've never been able to make it work long term, just the two of us, but maybe there's a solution.

Maybe he's right.

"How would we make it work?" I ask, not fully

knowing why the hell that's the first thing that comes out of my mouth.

Hayes lowers himself into the car and scoots over for me as I slide in beside him. He exchanges a quick hello with the driver, but then he tunes us out as he answers his phone. Hayes looks back at me. "I don't know. We'd just have to figure it out as we go."

I tilt my head to the side as the car pulls away from the curb. "That's the stupidest thing I've ever heard."

"Maybe it is," he says slowly, his voice trailing off before he gives me a devious grin. "Or maybe it's the best fucking idea yet." He pauses again. "I think I may have found our match, and I think you'd really like her."

I stare at him, waiting for him to continue because I have a feeling where he might be going with this now. "Who?"

"Do you remember Quinn?" he asks, looking at his phone to see how far we are from our destination before his gaze meets mine again. "The physical therapist I was telling you about?"

Jesus Christ.

Hayes has told me all about her and honestly, I've been intrigued since the moment he told me about the interactions and the tension between them. But that doesn't eliminate the fact that she works for the

Aston Archers—the very team Hayes plays for. He knows it and I know it.

Shit, we all know it.

It's a line he probably shouldn't cross.

"I remember."

That doesn't mean he won't cross it...

"She was at Matthews' party last night." Hayes stops talking as the driver pulls up and we both exit the vehicle. We fall into step beside each other as he starts to talk again. "We almost hooked up in his laundry room in the middle of the party."

"What happened?"

Hayes purses his lips as we pause outside of the entrance to the bar. "Fucking Ford came to the door because Nova was looking for me. You know how she gets everyone on the team something small for the holiday."

I nod, remembering the small handmade candle I found on the counter this morning when I woke up. "So, what happened with Quinn after that?"

Hayes shrugs and pulls open the door for me as I step inside the building. It's relatively empty, considering it's Christmas Day and most people are busy with their families. Hayes and I didn't have anywhere to go and it's one of the only places open in the outskirts of Aston.

"She hid in the cabinet and then I saw her in her

car a few minutes later," he tells me with amusement dancing in his tone. "I'm guessing she probably snuck out when no one was paying attention—probably right after we almost got caught."

I let out a laugh, shaking my head at him as we walk up to the bar and sit down beside one another. "Wait. She hid in the cabinet?"

A chuckle rumbles in his chest and he nods. "It was an in-the-moment decision, so no one saw us together. She hid in there and I went out with Ford to find Nova."

I stare at my best friend and roommate for a moment as I process the things he's telling me. He made out and almost hooked up with someone who works for the Archers and didn't talk to her afterward, yet he seems to think I would like her and she would be into both of us.

"You're delusional."

His eyebrows pull together as I blurt out the words. "Why?"

"What makes you think you found our match in her?" I tilt my head to the side at him before we're interrupted by the bartender. He sets two napkins in front of us and asks for our order.

Hayes orders each of us an old-fashioned before the bartender steps away to make our drinks.

"Did you tell her about me?" I ask him, my voice

semi-low as my gaze meets his again. "Did you tell her about us?"

"Well, no," he says matter-of-factly, as if none of that is a big deal. "We didn't really get a chance to talk specifics."

"This is exactly why you're delusional," I tell him, snorting again. "You know that not all women are into bisexual men and they're not all into being shared either."

Hayes pushes his shoulders back, straightening his spine as the muscle in his jaw momentarily tightens. The bartender sets our drinks in front of us and I watch Hayes as he lifts his to take a sip.

"There's something about Quinn," he says quietly, his voice filled with confidence. "If you were there last night, I have no doubt you wouldn't be thinking the same right now."

I lift my own glass, swallowing back a mouthful of the liquid as I feel the burn sliding down my throat. Hayes isn't a delusional person, even if it may seem like it in this moment. I can't help but believe him. He doesn't throw around suggestions like this if he doesn't mean it. His gaze doesn't waver and I know he means every word he says.

"Okay, I believe you," I admit, assuring him as I give him a swift nod. "But how do you test this theory?"

Hayes slowly does a survey of the place and I watch his expression transform as his eyes fix on something across the bar. His nostrils flare as he continues to stare. My gaze follows his, landing on someone sitting alone on the other side, sipping a martini as she scrolls on her phone. I've seen her before, only once when Hayes showed me a picture, but she has the kind of face you don't forget.

Quinn Sanders.

Hayes turns his head to look at me, and our gazes collide instantly. I watch the way his throat bobs as he swallows. A ghost of a smile dances across his perfectly plump lips—lips I know all too well.

"Santa decided to deliver on Christmas after all," he says with a smirk as he motions with his head in her direction. "Come with me," he tells me as he picks up his glass and rises to his feet. "Let's see if I was getting the right vibes from her or if I imagined it all."

CHAPTER FOUR
QUINN

"Well, if it isn't the woman of my dreams…"

My breath catches in my throat at the sound of his voice. I didn't even notice anyone else had walked into the bar and, frankly, I'm not sure how long he's even been here. As I slowly turn to look at him standing behind me, I realize he isn't alone.

I raise an eyebrow at the two of them, recognizing his roommate, who I've seen once or twice before. "Are you sure you don't mean nightmare?"

His roommate snorts and Hayes levels his gaze on mine. A fire burns brightly in his irises and the tension is immediately there, growing in the space between us. "Whatever you are, I'll take it."

A soft laugh escapes me and I shake my head as I

reach for my drink on the bar. "What are you guys doing here? You know it's Christmas, right?"

"Neither of our families live locally and Chase didn't feel like traveling, so I figured I'd stay home to keep him company." Hayes pauses, narrowing his eyes at me as he tilts his head to the side. "Why are you here? Weren't you supposed to be with your boyfriend for the holiday?"

Fuck.

For the past few minutes, I've forgotten Luke exists and that he humiliated me earlier today. The last thing I was expecting was having to explain it to anyone… and I know Hayes. He's not going to take the watered-down version, especially after the moment we shared last night.

"We broke up."

Hayes straightens his head, a wave of sympathy passing through his eyes as he frowns. "I'm sorry, Quinn. He's a fucking asshole."

"It sounds like it," Chase adds in, his deep voice vibrating against my eardrums. "That's a dick move to make on a holiday."

"Well, he didn't plan on doing it today," I say, a harsh laugh escaping me before I drain the rest of my martini and set the glass back on the bar. "He didn't realize I was coming. He was there with the girl he's been cheating on me with."

The muscle in Hayes's jaw twitches. "Where can I find this piece of shit?"

"Calm down, killer." I let out a breath, a smile pulling on my lips as I flatten my palm against his chest. "I was planning on breaking up with him anyways... this was just a little unexpected. He gave me an out, though, so really, I'm happy about it."

"It sounds like you're better off without him," Chase tells me, his eyes boring holes through my own as I rise to my feet. "It sounds like you need someone better."

I tilt my head to the side, my eyes roaming over his face as I study every inch of his attractive features. "Are you implying something?"

I don't know why the hell I said that. Probably from the alcohol, even though I'm not drunk. I have the lightest buzz, but it's enough to make me speak without thinking.

"Depends on if you want me to be or not."

My eyes travel to Hayes's before slowly bouncing back and forth between the two men. Hayes is watching the interaction between Chase and me, almost as if he's assessing the situation. Chase is still staring at me, waiting for me to make my next move.

"Hmm," I murmur, pushing past them as the music playing in the bar switches to something faster and more upbeat. Supposedly the best way to get over one man is to get under another. I wonder if that applies to two men.

Moving away from the bar, I let the music flow through my body, feeling the beat as my heart pounds in my chest. Lifting my arms above my head, I start to sway my hips, tipping my head back as my eyelids fall shut. I slowly turn around to face Hayes and Chase, my head moving back to a neutral position as I see them watching me.

"Do either of you dance?" I ask as I continue to move with the music, my hips shifting back and forth as my skirt shifts against my thighs. I wasn't planning my holiday around rebounding from Luke, but plans can change.

Hayes and Chase share a glance that I'm unable to decipher before directing their attention back to me. "We do," Chase says softly, but neither of them moves. "Sometimes we prefer to watch instead."

My stomach flutters, my heart skips a beat, and my breath hitches in my throat. *Okay…* Turning away from them, I start to move again, attempting to ignore the sound of his voice as his words linger in my mind. Closing my eyes again, I let myself drift away, getting lost in the music as I twist my body around.

I can feel Hayes entering my space as he steps up behind me. He doesn't touch me at first, but warmth radiates from his body, heating my backside. He lingers, almost as if he's not sure whether or not to make a move. My feet move as I spin around to face him. He's standing closer than I expected him to and I have to tilt my head back to look up at him.

"Hey."

The corners of his lips twitch. "Hey."

My heart pounds erratically in my chest as the electricity buzzes in the air between us. I'm not usually forward, but fuck it, right? If you want something, sometimes you have to just take a chance. And after the day I've had, I could really use a distraction.

Reaching for his hands, I lift them to my hips, letting them rest there as I step closer to him. Hayes's nostrils flare and his fingertips dig into my flesh as he holds on to me, moving his body with mine. "I was surprised to see you here," he murmurs, his voice low as he dips his face down to my ear. "I'd be lying if I said I wasn't happy to find out you're single."

I swallow roughly, lifting my arms to circle them around the back of his neck as warmth builds in the pit of my stomach. "Oh really?"

"Yeah."

I inhale sharply as he moves his head away, unlinking my arms before spinning me around to face the opposite direction. Chase is standing a few feet away, his eyes on us as he watches Hayes pressing his hips against me. His erection presses through his pants, rubbing against my ass as he moves with me.

"Does that change things for you now?" He breathes the words against my ear, his lips brushing against the outer shell.

My gaze is trained on Chase's as I shift my hips. Hayes runs his hands down my arms, reaching for my wrists before lifting my arms up to the back of his neck. I move closer to him, my tongue darting out to wet my lips. "It does."

"Let me be your rebound, Quinn," he says softly, nipping at my ear as he presses his cock against me. "And if you're into it, I'll even share you with him."

Jesus fuck. My mouth is instantly dry at the thought alone. I've never been with two guys before, but it's a fantasy I've always had. It's an experience I've always wanted to check off my list.

"Is that something the two of you are into?"

Hayes hums into my ear, his hips moving with mine. "It is," he admits, his voice hoarse with lust. Chase drains the rest of his drink and sets it down on the bar before he begins to move closer to us. "You see, Chase and I are kind of a package deal."

Chase tilts his head to the side, his gaze dropping to my lips as he can't hear what we're talking about. I have an idea of what Hayes is getting at, but I want to hear the words from him.

"Meaning what?"

"We'll share you…" He pauses, motioning for Chase to come to us. "But we also like to indulge in one another too."

Holy shit. I never thought I would be one of God's favorites, but it looks like the odds are in my favor today. The thought of these two men together sends a shiver down my spine. Again, it's a first for me, although it's another thing I've fantasized about before.

"Are you two together?" I ask him while also asking Chase.

Chase chuckles, half shrugging as he enters my space. "We don't really have any labels." The intensity in his gaze has me clenching my thighs together. He doesn't touch me and I find myself desperate to feel his hands too. "Neither of us are particularly interested in other men, but it's different with women."

"And you both want to be my rebound…"

Hayes spins me around to face him, his face inching closer to mine. "Do you have another way you'd like to spend your Christmas?"

My chest rises and falls in rapid succession, my body buzzing from the electricity between the three of us. My heart thumps against my rib cage and it stumbles over itself as I feel Chase's hands wrapping around my waist, just above Hayes's.

"The choice is yours, Quinn," Chase murmurs, his lips brushing against my left ear as Hayes's drift across my mouth. I feel Chase against me, the warmth rolling off his body. "We don't have to do anything you don't want to do."

What if I want to do it all?

Instinctively, I rub my ass against him, feeling how hard he is as he presses against me. A moan slips from my lips before I get the chance to control myself. "Not here," I mumble, the words tumbling from my lips in a rush. "Anyone could see us here."

"Right," Hayes says, pulling back. "What if I told you I don't care if anyone sees us?"

"Well, I'd rather not get caught and lose my job because of a random hookup."

He chuckles softly. "Nothing about this is random, Quinn."

Chase takes a step away from me and I immediately feel his absence. I glance over my shoulder at him, catching him looking at Hayes before looking at me. "Would you like to come back to our place?"

There isn't a single moment of hesitation.

"Yes."

Tonight is about taking what I want... and I want them.

CHAPTER FIVE
HAYES

"Did either of you drive?" Quinn questions Chase and I as we all step out onto the sidewalk. I paid for our tab and hers before we slipped out of the bar. She wraps her peacoat tighter around her body as we all come to a stop.

Chase shakes his head. "No, we figured there would be a bunch of cops out tonight so we just got an Uber here instead. Neither of us planned on getting drunk, but the last thing either of us needs is to get pulled over after having a few drinks.."

Quinn nods. "I'm not drunk either, but I agree with this idea. Better safe than sorry."

My phone is already out and I'm about to press the button for the car when I look at Quinn again. "If you don't want to come with us, we can get you a car to take you home. Neither of us want you to feel pressured or anything."

She stares at me for a moment, her expression unreadable before she smiles. "I want to. If I didn't, I wouldn't be standing here right now." She pauses and winks at me. "I know how to say no, Hayes."

I stare at her for a moment and her smile doesn't waver. My finger presses the button to secure our ride and a small box flashes up to show how far away the car is. Thankfully, it's only two minutes away from where we are, which is surprising considering the holiday.

Chase and Quinn fall into a comfortable conversation and I hang back, letting them get to know each other. They've never formally met before tonight and I want Quinn to feel at ease with both of us. The two of them laugh at something I don't catch. I smile in response, watching the way Quinn appears to be relaxed.

I know her well enough to read her body language. I also know that Quinn has no problem telling people like it is. If she wasn't interested, she would have put her foot down. She would have never entertained the thought.

I'm just glad she didn't feel the need to remind me again that we shouldn't be doing this. It's a fact we both know. As long as neither of us get caught, we don't have to worry about our jobs. Although, I'm not sure either of us would really get into any trouble anyway.

The car pulls up to the curb and Chase walks over first, pulling open the door. I slip inside first, scooting to the opposite side as Quinn follows suit, situating herself in the middle as Chase gets in last. Our driver confirms the location before he takes a call, tuning the three of us out.

Quinn stares straight ahead. "Am I allowed to ask the two of you some questions?"

"Of course," I tell her, my voice low as we all settle into our seats as he pulls away from the curb. "What would you like to know?"

"How long have you known each other?"

Chase answers this question. "Since college. We were roommates."

She pulls her bottom lip between her teeth, nodding as she looks over at him. "Were you guys together in college?"

"Not exactly," Chase admits to her. "We had a bi-awakening moment and ended up hooking up. We didn't again until after college."

"Why not?"

He shrugs. "Neither of us knew what we wanted at the time." It really wasn't complicated then and it still isn't. We're just older now and things have changed from our college years.

"Do you know what you want now?"

Chase looks past her and directly at me. "We do," I answer her question. She turns her head to look at me now. "We want each other, but we want someone who complements both of us. Someone who isn't opposed to it being the three of us."

Quinn stares at me, her slender throat bobbing as she swallows and nods. "It's unconventional," she says quietly before rolling her lips between her teeth. "And intriguing."

"You don't have to worry about any of that right now, Doc," I assure her, feeling the need to make sure there isn't any pressure. "Tonight is just about discovery and experience. If it feels like something you'd like to explore more afterward, that's a conversation we can have at another time."

"So, this is like test driving a car in a way," she offers, a soft laugh escaping her as she looks back and forth between Chase and I. "Am I the car?"

Chase laughs, shaking her head at her. "It goes both ways."

The tension is building, but there's a lightness to the mood. There isn't any awkwardness. Her curiosity is honestly refreshing. She's trying to figure us out and understand the way we operate, without any judgment. None of us know if this is going to be a good fit, but every participant is ready to find out.

"You know," I start, my voice dropping lower so only they can hear as I set my hand on her bare thigh. Her skin is warm beneath my palm and I slowly trail my hand along the inside of her leg. "I've been thinking about you for a long fucking time, Doc."

"Since before last night?" she asks me, her breath hitching as I slip my hand beneath the hem of her skirt. Chase watches the two of us as he lifts his hand to brush her blonde hair away from her collarbone.

The driver has no fucking clue what's going on as he rambles on the phone, staring out the window as we stop at a red light.

"Yes," I tell her, my fingers brushing against her center. "Probably since the first time I ever laid eyes on you."

"I've been curious about you since he first mentioned you."

She glances at Chase as he drops his hand down to her opposite thigh. "He told you about me?"

"He tells me everything, pretty girl," he tells her with a wink as he mimics my movements, his fingertips brushing against mine as we both explore between her legs. "Are you okay with this?"

She pulls her bottom lip between her teeth, spreading her legs wider as she adjusts in her seat.

Her breathing is shallow and ragged and she glances between us before nodding. Chase hooks his finger in her panties, pulling them to the side for me to explore.

She's already wet and my cock pulsates between my legs as I slide my finger through the dampness. I swallow back the groan that builds in my throat. My nostrils flare as I watch her eyelids flutter shut and I push my finger inside of her. Her shoulders sag and she lets out a breath, her eyes flying open again as she looks toward the front of the car.

"He has no fucking clue," Chase murmurs as he moves his fingers to her clit. "And if you're quiet, he'll never know."

Quinn nods eagerly as her hands find both of our thighs. Her nails dig into my flesh through my pants as I slip another finger inside of her. I glance at the driver and out the window, realizing we will be at our place soon.

"We'll be there in less than two minutes," I tell her, pumping my fingers in and out of her as Chase rolls his fingers over her clit. "Do you think we can make you come before we get there?"

"I don't know," she whispers, attempting to steady her breathing even though she's close to coming undone. "I don't think you should stop trying."

Chase clicks his tongue as he stalls. His hand is still against her, but he doesn't move. "I think we should make her wait," he tells me, a glint in his eye.

A chuckle rumbles in my chest as I stop moving. "We should." I pump my fingers deliberately slow. Chase rolls his again, but neither of us are in a rush. The car turns onto our street and we both move our hands away from her.

"You've got to be fucking kidding me," Quinn groans before letting out an exaggerated sigh. "You're really going to leave me hanging?"

"For now," I tell her with a wink. "Good things come to good girls who wait patiently."

"Fuck your patience," she quips, glaring at the two of us.

Chase fixes her skirt before leaning closer to her. "We're going to fuck yours."

CHAPTER SIX
QUINN

The car pulls into a driveway that loops around the front of a massive building. Hayes leans forward, handing the driver a cash tip before we slip out of the back seat. The cold night air slides up my legs, a stark contrast to the damp warmth that's between my legs. I have the two of them to thank for that, after they almost made me come and decided to edge me instead.

Hayes walks up to the door first, holding up a key until there's a loud buzzing sound and a click as the lock opens. He reaches for the handle, pulling it open in one swift, fluid movement. I look over at him and he smirks at me. Following Chase, I walk into the lobby of the building with Hayes hot on my heels.

His hands find my hips as we move over to the

elevator and he pulls me flush against his front as he drapes his arms over my shoulders. He's much taller than me, enveloping me as he buries his face in the crook of my neck.

Chase watches the two of us with a blazing heat in his irises. Hayes's cock presses against my lower back and I push my ass against him, a hearty moan spilling from his lips. The sound vibrates against my neck, sending a warmth straight to the place between my legs. The elevator reaches the floor and dings as the doors slide open.

Hayes releases me, letting me walk on my own as we step inside. Chase faces me as Hayes stands behind him, pressing the button for the twenty-third floor. My breath catches in my throat as Chase closes the distance between us, not stopping until his feet reach mine and he's pinning me up against the cool metal wall.

His mouth meets mine in an instant. There isn't a single ounce of hesitation or restraint. His lips are soft and warm, but there's nothing tender about the way he kisses me. There's a fervent need driving his movements. Lifting my hands, I grip the front of his shirt, needing to feel him closer, but the only way to do that is if he's naked.

His tongue slides along the seam of my lips and I part them, letting him in. There's a shift in intensity.

A moan escapes me and he swallows the sound as our tongues tangle together. His hands are in my hair, pulling my head back farther as he swallows me whole. Any coherent thought evades me. He surrounds me, consuming me as he kisses me intently.

Hayes's hand brushes the side of my face, momentarily startling me. A gasp escapes me, my breath hitching as he trails his fingers down the side of my neck, dancing them across my collarbone before they begin their descent along the curve of my breast that's exposed by my low-cut shirt.

"I hate to be the bearer of bad news, but we're at our floor."

Chase smiles against my lips as he begins to break away. He lets out a soft hum and turns his head to look at Hayes, his arms still caging me in. "It sounds like someone's a little jealous." He pushes off the wall, taking a step back before he looks at me. "Who do you think he's more jealous of?"

A low rumble vibrates in Hayes's chest as he lifts his hand and grabs Chase's chin, jerking his head to the side to look back at him. "I'm not jealous," he promises, his face inching closer to Chase's. "Impatient, yes, but there's no need to be jealous when I know I'm going to have both of you soon enough."

My back is still pressed against the wall and my

mouth is dry as I watch the two of them, feeling the tension rolling off them in waves. Time is momentarily suspended, the electricity crackling in the air around us as I wait for one of them to make the first move.

Neither of them does.

Hayes releases Chase's chin and my chest deflates with disappointment as Hayes turns around and walks out of the elevator first. Chase looks back at me, his nostrils flaring before a smirk lifts his lips. "Come on," he says with a wink, holding his hand out to me. "If you dare."

The elevator took us directly to their floor and the moment I step out, I'm standing in the foyer of their home. I follow suit, kicking off my heels after I see Chase and Hayes leaving their shoes by the door. Hayes disappears around the corner and Chase glances at me.

"I promise neither of us bite," he tells me with a smirk. "That is, unless that's something you're into."

"How about you get me a drink and then I'll tell you what I'm into," I retort, winking at him before he pulls me toward the kitchen.

Hayes steps out into the living room and fiddles with the speaker system as I watch Chase make three mixed drinks. Music starts to play through the condo and a smile pulls at my lips. I've always loved to dance and tonight at the bar was the first time in a long time.

Chase hands me my drink, leading the way into the living room as he hands Hayes his. They stand off to the side, and I begin to walk around, surveying their space as I look at the minimal decorations. It looks like they got it furnished or had someone decorate for them.

Along the mantle are a few family pictures, but none of them with anyone else. I smile as I look at the ones of Hayes with his parents and Chase and his siblings. It's sweet, really, and the personal touches add more to the room.

The song finishes and changes to the next one and I can't help myself. "Oh, I love this song!" I spin on my heel, finding them watching me as I start to move my body to the music.

Chase leans against the doorway, a curious look on his face as he slowly lifts his glass to his lips. He stays silent as he watches me with an intensity that has my insides growing warm.

Hayes stands off to the side of him, his gaze trained on me. "Are you going to put on a show for us, Doc?"

Closing my eyes, I tip my head back and let the

music flow through my body as I begin twisting and swaying to the beat. If they want a show, I'll give them one…

One that's going to have these two men begging on their knees for me.

CHAPTER SEVEN
CHASE

Leaning against the doorframe, I lift my glass to my lips, the burn of the liquor sliding down my throat as I watch Quinn dancing in the center of the living room. She's holding her glass above her head, her body swaying to the rhythm of the music. Her head tilts back, her hips shifting to the sound. I glance over at Hayes who's as transfixed on her as I am.

Time drifts away as I watch the way he watches her. Quinn straightens her head and she sees Hayes first. She lifts her hand into the air and crooks her finger, signaling for him to come to her as she continues to move to the melody. Hayes glances over at me, a dark, mischievous look passing over his eyes as Quinn glances at me, motioning for me to come too.

I don't move from where I'm standing and watch as Hayes stalks over to her. He steps up behind her, his hands instantly finding her hips as he pulls her back against him. My eyes fall to her ass, watching the way she grinds it against him. Hayes drops his mouth down to her neck, his lips trailing along the side before stopping by her ear.

My cock is harder than a fucking rock, pressing against my pants. It pulsates, throbbing with need as my eyes are trained on Hayes and Quinn in front of me. Quinn says something but it's not loud enough for me to hear. The music is too loud, drowning out her voice. He lifts his head, dragging his tongue along the side of her throat as his eyes meet mine. My dick feels like it's going to combust at any moment.

His lips brush against her ear as he whispers something to her. The corners of her lips lift and she motions for me to come to them again.

Pushing away from the doorway, I drain the rest of my drink before setting it on the side table next to the couch. My feet carry me across the room toward them, my body buzzing from the adrenaline pumping through my veins. Both of their gazes are on me as I stalk closer, stopping directly in front of Quinn as Hayes sways behind her. A sultry smile transforms her lips as my eyes travel between the two of them, mesmerized as their bodies melt together.

"Do you want to join us?" she asks, her hands tentatively reaching out to cup the sides of my face as she urges me closer.

I stare directly at her, the corners of my mouth twitching. "Do you want me to?"

Hayes stares back at me, his jaw clenched as he runs his hands along the sides of Quinn's torso. "Do you want us to share you, Doc?"

"Mm," she murmurs, rocking her hips against him as she pulls me flush against her so she's sandwiched between us. She tips her head back, her gaze hooded as I trail my fingers along the column of her throat. "I've never been shared before," she whispers, her breath warm against my lips as my face dips down toward hers.

"We don't have to if you don't want to."

"I do," she breathes, letting out a soft moan as I press my erection against her. "I want you both."

My fingers slide around her neck, wrapping around them as my lips crash to hers. Hayes slides his hands up her sides, inching her shirt farther up her body as he nips and sucks the flesh on her neck. His mouth trails over my hand, tasting my skin as if it's a part of Quinn, but we both know it's not.

A groan rises from my throat, my cock straining

even harder against my pants as my tongue slips inside Quinn's mouth. She tastes sweet like the wine she was drinking and I want to lose myself in her. In him. In them. She moves her lips in tandem with mine, her tongue sliding across mine before she nips at my bottom lip.

Hayes wraps his hand around mine, pulling me away from Quinn as he lifts her shirt. We break apart, only momentarily as he peels the soft silk away from her torso and unhooks her bra. Quinn drops her hands from my waist, letting the straps slide down her arms until it's falling onto the floor by her feet.

His arms slip back around her waist, pulling her back against him as my eyes travel across the planes of her body, drinking in the sight of her. "Fuck," I murmur, my gaze trailing over her pebbled nipples.

"You want him to touch you, Doc?" Hayes asks her, his voice low as he drags his fingers under the waistband of her skirt.

"Yes," she breathes, her eyes meeting mine as she tilts her head back, her lips parting slightly. "I want to feel both of you on my skin. Touch me, Chase."

Jesus fucking Christ.

Her face is flushed, her plump lips already parted for me. A shaky breath falls from her mouth, her chest rising and falling in rapid succession. I wonder which one of us will be the first to sink deep inside her.

"Beg for it."

Hayes's heated gaze is on me, but I don't look away from Quinn. Stepping closer to her, I slide my thumb and forefinger under her jaw. My other hand begins its journey, lightly touching Hayes's as I stroke her stomach for a brief second before pulling my hand away. I raise an eyebrow, tilting my head as I wait.

"Please, Chase," her plea is soft and breathless, "I want your hands on me, your skin on mine. I need you to touch me."

My hands are back on her as our mouths collide. Cupping both of her breasts in my hands, I knead her flesh between my fingers, pulling and twisting her nipples. I swallow the soft sigh that falls from her lips. Quinn grinds her ass against Hayes as he kisses the side of her neck. Her tongue is inside my mouth, tasting and teasing.

Her skin is so soft and warm under my palms, but I need more. I need to feel him too. My hands abandon her breasts as my tongue swirls in her mouth and my arms drape over her back, reaching out to him.

Hayes inhales sharply as my fingertips graze the skin on his lower abdomen. My hands slide under his shirt, pushing it upward as I trail my fingers along the ridges of his muscles.

"Chase," he moans my name against the side of Quinn's neck, which only seems to encourage her. She kisses me deeper, her hands fisting the collar of my shirt. "Fuck…"

Warmth spreads through my body and I pull away from Quinn, my eyes bouncing between hers and Hayes's. I step away, giving them one last glance. "My bedroom. Now."

Spinning on my heel, I pull my shirt over my head, tossing it onto the floor as I walk down the small hallway to my room. I hear Hayes and Quinn behind me as I unbutton my pants, letting them hang open before I walk over to my bed and turn around to face the doorway. Quinn pulls Hayes into the room, stopping just outside my door as she lets go of him. My eyes widen as she reaches for the waistband of her skirt, unzipping it before it falls to the floor.

She stands in front of us, hooking her fingers under the string of her thong before she bends over and slides them down her legs. Her eyes meet mine as she stands back upright. Hayes is behind her, stripping out of his own clothes as Quinn steps up to me.

Her hands find my pants and she pushes them down my thighs, dragging my boxer briefs along with them. My cock springs free as she strips me of my clothing.

"That's better," she murmurs, a smirk forming on her face as her heavy eyes meet mine. "Much better."

I watch her with a heated gaze and I direct it to Hayes as he steps into the room completely naked. My eyes travel along the length of his body, the thickness of his cock that I vividly remember, before turning my attention back to Quinn. Hayes walks past us, dropping down onto my bed, and scoots up toward the headboard as he settles flat on his back.

Quinn's hips sway as she walks over to the side of the bed, glancing back and forth between the two of us. "What now?" she asks us both, her voice quiet and hesitant. This isn't the first time Hayes and I shared someone, but goddamn, it feels like a first.

"Come here," Hayes tells her, his hand reaching for her thigh as he urges her toward the bed. "Come sit on my face."

An anxious look crosses her face for a moment, but then her inhibitions vanish in an instant as her high clearly overrides any hesitation that she was feeling. Quinn doesn't say another word, her lips lifting upward as she climbs onto the bed. She hovers over Hayes, positioning herself on top of him. My eyelids feel heavy and my balls ache as I watch her lowering her pussy to his mouth.

I'm still standing at the foot of the bed and my hand finds my cock as Quinn grabs onto the headboard. Hayes slides his hands around her thighs, grabbing her ass as he holds her in place. I watch the way his mouth opens, his tongue sliding out to lick her. Quinn moans softly, her hips bucking as he starts to fuck her with his mouth. I grip myself tighter, stroking the length of my dick as I begin to pump my hand.

Quinn moans softly, her hips shifting as Hayes holds her in place, devouring her. Her head falls back in ecstasy and I resist the urge to climb onto the bed with them. I want to watch this moment. I want to see him pleasuring her.

"Chase." Quinn's voice is hoarse as she breathes my name into the room. Her body twists slightly but her pussy doesn't leave his mouth. "Come here."

I clear my throat, my eyes glued to hers as I climb onto the bed. The mattress dips beneath my weight and I pause on my knees behind her, directly in between Hayes's legs. "I'm here."

"Touch him," she breathes as she lets out a quiet laugh. "I want to watch you touch him."

Fuck. I've never had someone tell me what to do with Hayes before and this is hot as fucking hell.

"What do you want me to do to him?"

Hayes growls against Quinn's pussy, his mouth

moving faster as he continues to eat her. Her hips buck, grinding against his face as she lets out another moan. My fingertips graze Hayes's thighs, beginning their journey toward his cock. I don't stop, my palms sliding against his flesh until I'm brushing against his erection. Hayes groans, his hips shifting as I wrap my hand around his shaft.

"Suck his cock," Quinn pants, riding his face as he pushes his tongue inside her. "Suck him until he comes."

A groan rumbles in Hayes's chest as I start to pump my hand. A devious grin slides across Quinn's lips as she watches me over her shoulder as I lower my head down toward his dick. My eyes don't leave hers as my tongue darts out and I run the tip along the underside of his cock. Hayes's grip tightens on Quinn's ass and they simultaneously moan as I wrap my lips around the tip of him.

My mouth stretches around him as I slide myself down, inhaling the entire length of his cock until the head slides down the back of my throat, cutting off my breathing. Tears spring to my eyes and the muscles in my throat constrict around him as I gag. Deep throating him was always something I struggled with, but it's been so long. It's exactly where I want him.

I hear the sharp intake of Hayes's breath before

his hips lift against me. Quinn grinds against Hayes's mouth and her hands find the headboard as she holds on. She turns her head away from me, lost in her own pleasure as her eyelids fall shut and her head tilts back. My lips are suctioned around Hayes's cock, the head bouncing against the back of my throat with every thrust.

Every time my head bobs and I swallow him, Hayes lifts his hips to meet me, effectively fucking my throat at the same time I'm sucking his dick. I drop my other hand to his balls, wrapping my fingers around him as I start to massage them. They constrict, drawing closer to his body as I keep sliding him in and out of my mouth.

My own dick is throbbing, begging for attention, but I know that will come later. I'll get my turn. Right now, all I care about is making him come while he makes her come. The room is filled with the sounds of them moaning and the wetness of his tongue lapping her pussy while I keep sucking him. Quinn cries out and I lift my gaze to her, watching her body writhing on top of him. Her thighs tighten around the sides of his face and her back arches as she moans both of our names loudly.

Her orgasm consumes her body, sending shock waves through her as she jerks around on Hayes's face. I hold him tighter, his hips lifting faster as I take him in deep. I don't stop, fucking him with my mouth, letting him bruise the back of my throat with the head of his cock.

Hayes groans, my name escaping his lips as he moans it against Quinn's cunt while his own orgasm takes over. He falls over the edge, his hips shifting faster when I taste him in the back of my tongue. I take him in deeper, tasting the saltiness of him, swallowing every spurt of cum. He tastes just like I remember. I slow down my movements as I suck him dry. Hayes releases his grip on Quinn's ass and finds my hair instead.

He weaves his fingers through my locks, gripping me tightly until there's nothing left. My throat aches and I feel like I'm about to come just from watching, feeling, and tasting them. Quinn climbs off Hayes as I slowly pull my mouth away from his cock. My eyes meet Hayes's as he scoots farther up the bed, sitting up with his head against the headboard. I lift my hand, wiping the wetness from my lips with the back of it. My throat bobs as I swallow again, still tasting him on my tongue.

A ghost of a smile dances across his lips.

Quinn's sitting on the bed, half between us as she looks from Hayes and back to me. It's almost as if she's trying to assess the situation. They're still floating on a fucking high and I'm ready to chase mine. Quinn inches closer to me, reaching for my shoulders as she gently pushes me onto my back in the center of the bed.

Hayes moves his legs out of the way and watches as Quinn swings her leg over me, straddling me. My cock is throbbing, begging for a release. I don't miss the way Hayes drags his eyes over my body, taking his time as he re acquaints himself with every inch he's touched and tasted before.

Quinn hovers above me and she reaches between us, wrapping her delicate hand around the shaft of my cock. She lifts it, positioning it so the head of my dick is pressing against her swollen, soaked pussy. She plants her other hand on my chest as I grab her hips. Her movements are deliberately slow as she lowers herself onto me, taking the entire length of me deep inside her tight pussy as she sits down on me.

A groan rumbles in my chest, my eyes practically rolling back in my head as Quinn moans. She feels fucking amazing wrapped around me. Hayes moves off the bed and stands to the side. His eyes are transfixed on us, watching as she starts to rock her hips. I start to lift her up the length of my cock before letting her drop back down onto me.

Quinn takes over and begins to move on her own, sliding up and down. I look behind her at Hayes who's watching us with need burning deep within his dark irises. Quinn's head tips back, her neck fully exposed as she gets lost in her pleasure again. She doesn't need either of us to do it for her right now. She's the one who's in control and she has every intention of taking it.

I only let her have her moment for so long before I start to take over again. I top her from the bottom when I feel her body starting to grow tired. My hands grip her hips and Hayes's nostrils flare as I glance down at his hard cock. I lift Quinn up and drop her back down as I thrust my own hips. My tongue darts out to wet my lips as I stare at Hayes.

As much as I want her... I want him too.

In the bedroom, I like to exercise my control, and I want Hayes to hand it over to me.

"Come on, Hayes," I breathe, my voice low and hoarse as my eyes travel back up to his. Ecstasy rolls through my body, washing over me completely. Lust and need fill the air between us. "I know you love to watch, but I know you love to join too."

Quinn turns her head to look back at him as I still her, holding her against my groin with my cock filling her completely. "Come here," Quinn's voice is like a melody and it fucks my eardrums when she tempts him. "Show me what the two of you do when you share."

Hayes moves closer to her and she reaches for

him as I lift my hips, pressing into her deeper. Her eyelids flutter as a moan escapes her. "Tell me what to do."

"I want you both to fuck me at the same time," Quinn moans, grinding against me as she lifts her hands to tug on her nipples.

"Fuck her ass," I command, my voice thick and hoarse with lust. Warmth floods my body, and my cock grows harder than humanly possible. "I wanna feel your cock rubbing against mine inside her."

Hayes looks from me to Quinn. Her blue eyes are glazed over as she looks at him over her shoulder. "You want that, Doc?" he asks her, his voice low and quiet, throaty, and filled with need. "You want to feel both of us inside you at the same time?"

"Mmmm," she hums, her lips pressed together as I lift her along my length before thrusting my cock back inside her. "I want you to fuck me together."

Hayes positions himself on his knees, approaching her from behind. I part my legs farther, granting him access as he slips between my thighs. He slides a finger into her pussy, earning a moan from her as he pumps it alongside my cock, coating it with her wetness. Quinn leans forward, moaning again as he removes his finger and slides it into her ass. She lets out a gasp, her breasts crushing against my chest as her face contorts.

"Oh my god," she breathes, half panting as he stretches her with his finger, just enough to make room for himself. He pulls his finger out of her once more, spitting into his hand before he fists his cock.

"Are you sure this is what you want?" I ask her, my cock slamming into her once more. "We don't have to go any further if you don't want to."

"This is what I want," she assures me, lifting her face to stare down at me. "I don't want either of you to stop."

"You're ours, Quinn," Hayes growls as he fists his cock, coating it with his saliva. "After this, you belong to us."

"Yes." Quinn inhales sharply, her body lifting slightly as Hayes begins to ease into her. "Own me. Ruin me." Her nostrils flare, her breathing growing shallow and erratic as he starts to move behind her, stretching her to fit around him.

Releasing my hand, I slide it between our bodies, my fingers finding her clit as she stares at me wide-eyed. Her lips part and a ragged breath escapes her. "Relax, baby," I murmur, rolling my finger over her to work her out of the nervous state she's in. "Let him in. Let us both in."

Quinn swallows hard, nodding as she lets out another breath. She starts to relax as Hayes starts to move with more urgency inside of her. Hayes's hands grip her ass, spreading her cheeks apart as he pushes himself farther into her. I grab the bottom of Quinn's chin, pulling her face down to mine. Our mouths collide, lips parting, teeth clashing, tongues tangling.

She kisses me deeply with an intensity that rocks me to my core. She cries out as Hayes fills her and I swallow the sound as I continue to move my fingers over her clit. Her tongue dances with mine and I feel her relaxing even more as Hayes falls into a steady rhythm. I wait to move until she's ready to handle both of us moving together.

Quinn pulls her mouth from mine and she stares down at me, letting out a soft moan while pleasure twists her expression. I feel Hayes's cock inside her and I lift her up to take over. We're both gentler, taking our time as we start to move in tandem together. I hold Quinn in place, lifting my hips to fuck her as Hayes fucks her ass.

"You good, Doc?" Hayes pants, his voice strained as he tightens his grip on her ass.

Quinn nods, her voice caught in her throat. She stares down at me, her eyes glazed over, as if she's lost in pure ecstasy as I continue to thrust my hips. I fill her to the hilt, each time feeling like it's deeper than the last as Hayes slides in and out of her backside.

"Fuck, look at you taking both of us at the same time," I groan, my fingers digging into her flesh. "You're a greedy little slut, aren't you? Greedy for both of our cocks to fill you at the same time."

"Let him hear you, Quinn," Hayes growls, nipping at the side of her neck with his lips and teeth. "Give him your words. Let him know how good it feels with both of us fucking you at the same time."

Hayes moves one hand, his shoulder shifting backward as he moves his arm behind his hip. I can't see what he's doing, but I feel it as soon as he grabs my balls with his hand. He massages them between his fingers and palm, sending a shock of electricity through my body as I slam my cock into Quinn.

"Fuck, Hayes," I moan, my voice hoarse. "Give me your words, Quinn."

Hayes's hips buck as he fills her even more, thrusting deep into her ass until we're both filling her to the brim. I can feel his cock through her pussy and I can't help myself as I moan with her.

"Jesus Christ, don't stop," Quinn pants as she starts to come apart at the seams. "I want you both to fuck me until you fill me with your cum."

I chuckle, the sound rumbling in my chest. "We're not going to stop until our cum is spilling from every fucking hole in your body."

Hayes's thrusts become harder and a moan escapes me as I match his energy, meeting him thrust for thrust. We're going to break her into a million fucking pieces, but Quinn doesn't seem like she would mind. She's too far gone, too encapsulated by the euphoria that's spreading through her body.

"Fuck, I'm going to come," Hayes groans, fucking her ass in the same rhythm as I slide into her pussy. "Goddammit. Come with me, Chase. Fill her with your cum while I fill her ass."

"You want that?" I ask her, my fingertips digging into her flesh as I bruise her skin. "You're so fucking wet for us, aren't you? Our little fucking slut."

"Fuck, don't stop," she breathes. Her head falls back, her eyes slamming shut. Her orgasm hits her out of nowhere and at full force as it violently courses through her like an electrical current.

She cries out, her pussy clenching around me while her ass simultaneously tightens around Hayes. She's a mess of moans, her body shaking, quivering, and rocking. Hayes and I keep moving, thrusting harder and harder into her until we both reach the peak. His cock strokes mine through her insides and she clenches around me like a vise grip.

My balls constrict and I shoot my cum into her, my hips pumping with each spurt until there's nothing left. At some point Quinn collapses against my chest and I wrap my arms around her, holding her close as I slow my movements. Hayes pulls out of her, both of our cum dripping from her holes as I ease myself out too.

I roll Quinn onto the bed and she gives me a lazy grin, fully satiated and filled with our cum. "Look at you," I murmur, pressing my lips to her temple as I ease off the bed. "You did so fucking good taking both of us at the same time."

Hayes disappears from the room for a few moments before he returns with a warm washcloth to clean her up with. Quinn reaches for us when he finishes. Words aren't needed as she pulls us onto the bed with her. We each lie on either side of her, sandwiching her between us as Hayes's and my arms snake around her body.

I like her here.

I like her with us.

CHAPTER EIGHT
QUINN

Hayes is gone when I wake up and Chase is still sleeping. My movements are deliberately slow and I'm silent as I try to crawl out of bed. Chase's arm immediately moves over my body and he pulls me back to him, pulling me flush against his chest.

"Where are you running off to?" Chase murmurs against the side of my neck as I move against him.

"I was trying to sneak away while you were still asleep."

He chuckles softly. "Nice try." He pauses for a moment before rolling me over to face him on the bed. He lifts his hand, running his thumb against my bottom lip. "Do you want me to let you run away?"

My throat bobs and I swallow roughly as I shake my head. Last night was supposed to be a one-night kind of thing, yet I find myself wanting more. I don't want to run away from him or Hayes. I want to stay right here to see what happens next.

"Then spend the day here with me. Hayes will be back later and maybe if he's lucky, you'll still be here then."

I stare at him for a moment, my eyes searching his as I watch lust swirling in his irises. We're close, so fucking close that I can feel the warmth of his cock as he presses his hips against mine. "I'll stay."

He slowly slides his hand down my throat, resting it on my collarbone. "I like that."

"I like you," I murmur, taking my chance as I move his hand away and push on his shoulders. Chase submits, rolling onto his back as I roll with him and straddle his lap. We're both already naked and I feel him pressing against me.

Chase lets out a low chuckle as he grabs my hips and flips me off of him. He shifts with me, moving me onto my back as he hovers above me. "What do you think Hayes would say if he walked in on us?"

I try to move beneath him. "I don't think he'd say anything," I tell him, attempting to wrap my legs around his waist to pull him closer, but he pushes me away. "I think he'd join in."

"Would you let both of us fuck you again?"

My mouth is instantly dry. "Yes."

"Fuck," he groans, his hips pressing against me. His eyes probe mine once more before he suddenly abandons his position and moves down my torso. He pushes my thighs apart. "Goddamn, you're perfect."

I stare back down at Chase, his perfect face settled between my legs. His words vibrate through my body and he closes his eyes as his head dips back down, licking along my center. He's skilled with his tongue, working himself against me in a way that has me gripping his hair in my hands and throwing my head back in pure ecstasy.

There's no comparison between him and Hayes, each of them is different in their own way, but in some ways they're both so similar. They both have the same effect on me, the same ability to make me a panting fucking mess as I chant their names like I'm praying to the stars above.

His hands creep up my body as he moves his tongue around my clit, licking and sucking as he pushes me closer and closer to the edge. He cups my bare breasts, kneading my flesh in his palms as he takes my nipples between his fingertips. He clamps down, tugging on them roughly as he devours me with his mouth.

I can't take it. There's an aspect that's forbidden, even though Hayes wouldn't care. I can't help but feel like we shouldn't be doing this without him here but with the way Chase eats me alive, my body has other fucking thoughts.

He fucks me with his mouth, using his arms to pin me down as I fight against him, my hips involuntarily bucking against his face. It doesn't take long before the warmth is spreading through my body, my climax steadily approaching. Chase doesn't stop, keeping the same rhythm as he fucks me to his own beat with just his tongue. One last swipe, one last swirl around my clit, and I'm turning into putty under his touch.

My hips buck as my orgasm tears through my body with such intensity that my legs begin to shake. I can't stop it as I throw my head back, screaming out in ecstasy. Chase's name falls from my lips, sounding more like a whisper as I struggle to catch my breath. My legs attempt to clamp around his head, but he moves his arms and pins them down with his weight, holding me still in place as he continues to devour me.

It's more than I can take and my body erupts as I burn alive under him. My hands are fisted in his dark hair and I'm trying to pull him away as he licks every drop of my orgasm from me. My pussy tingles to the point where the pain is mixing with the pleasure. My head's spinning, lost in the goddamn clouds, and I don't think I'm ever coming down.

Chase finally submits, lifting his head away from between my legs as he looks up at me with a smirk on his face. "I love the way you taste."

"Is that what you tell all the girls you go down on?" I level my gaze at him, challenging him, before looking at his chin that is damp with my cum. I love the way he looks right now, but my insecurities momentarily invade the moment.

"Nope," he says, his lips popping around the P sound. He slowly lifts himself up, wiping at his mouth with the back of his hand as he moves off the bed. "Normally, I don't go down on them. And if I do, I don't keep them around long enough for there to be room to exchange words." He stares at me for a moment, standing completely naked at the side of the bed.

My eyes fall to his cock and my insecurities immediately vanish. Those stupid thoughts are the furthest thing from my mind. My eyes widen for a beat. I swear to Christ, he's bigger than I remembered him being last night. "Oh god."

He smirks. "I like how that sounds."

"You're cocky as hell."

Chase lowers himself down onto the bed, pushing my legs apart again as he moves in between my thighs. "Not cocky, baby. Just confident."

I look down between us, my eyes trying to measure his length just from looking at him.

How the hell did I have both of them inside me at the same time?

Chase grips my chin, pressing my head back against the mattress as he looks down at me. "What's going on, Quinn? If you don't want to do this, we don't have to."

"No." I shake my head, my voice quiet. "I just—I don't think you're going to fit."

A chuckle vibrates from his chest and he smiles down at me. "You do know that this isn't our first time… right?"

"I know, but, like, I just don't know how that happened. What if we all just imagined it?"

He tilts his head to the side. "Hmmm… I don't think any of us imagined it."

I swallow roughly, my hands finding his hips as I urge him forward. His cock is hard against me and he slowly thrusts forward, splitting me wide open. He slides inside me effortlessly, filling me to the brim. My eyes slam shut, a moan slipping from my lips. "Okay, I think you fit."

"You remember me now, baby? Because your body sure as hell does."

As he rocks inside of me, memories of the night before with the three of us flash through my mind.

The way Hayes was so attentive. The way Chase made sure I was good, even when he was topping me from the bottom. Having him between my legs, with him on top, he's exactly where he belongs.

Chase stares down at me, a mix of emotion in his eyes, but I can't quite pick out a single one. They swirl in his blue irises and it's a similar look to the one that I've seen him give Hayes. My lips part slightly as he slowly rocks into me again, but he quickly silences me as his mouth collides with mine. He steals the air from my lungs as he inhales me, his tongue sliding against mine in one fluid movement.

He cups the side of my face with one hand as the other slides down the length of my torso, stopping as he reaches my hip. He gently grips my flesh, holding on to me as he begins his slow torture, easing himself in and out with precision. There's nothing rushed about his movements, no urgency behind them. He's taking his time with me and he's letting it be known.

His lips move against mine, melting against my skin as his tongue tangles with mine. There's no urgency behind his kiss either, although his mouth bruises mine with the force that he's struggling to hold back. Chase has a thing for control and right now, he has me under his thumb. I'm under his spell, lost in his charm, and he knows it.

But he doesn't take advantage of me. He's as lost

as I am, as curious as me, and willing to explore whatever this is that is growing between us. I can only hope Hayes feels the same way…

I open my mouth wider, deepening the kiss as I challenge him, pushing my tongue into his mouth. Chase growls against me, knowing exactly what I'm doing. As much as I like this tender side of him—I want to feel him—and I mean really *feel* him.

Chase pulls away slightly, planting his hand on the mattress beside my head as he slides his other hand under my ass, gripping my flesh in his palm. His fingertips dig into my skin and I moan quietly as I stare up into his bright blue eyes.

"I'm sorry, was I going too slow for you?" A ghost of a smile plays on his lips. "You want me to fuck you, don't you, baby?"

"Mhm," I murmur, running my nails down his back and digging into his skin. Wrapping my legs around his torso, I lift myself up, taking him in deeper.

"That's all you had to say, Quinn. Whatever you want, all you have to do is ask."

I slowly lick my lips, running my hands across his shoulders. "Fuck me, Chase. I want to feel you in my fucking rib cage."

His lips curl upward. "You're going to feel me long after we're done."

He moves both of his hands, grabbing my thighs and unwrapping my legs from around him. I straighten my knees as he positions my legs along the length of his body. My feet are on either side of his head and I link my ankles around the back of his neck for added support.

His hands are rough, gripping my ass as he positions himself on his knees, lifting me into the air to give himself a deeper angle. His fingertips dig into my flesh and my hips are suspended in the air as he slowly eases out of me before slamming back inside me. The tip of his cock hits my cervix and I cry out, the feeling a mixture of pleasure and pain.

The sounds that come from me only fuel him more, a dark expression consuming his face as a fire burns in his eyes. His gaze is glued to mine as he pistons his hips, driving his cock in and out of me with such force, my teeth knock together.

Chase strokes my insides with his length, filling me to the hilt as he continues to pound into me, fucking me relentlessly. I reach down, sliding my hand beneath me as I reach for his balls. Cupping them in my hand, I massage them, feeling them constrict as he picks up the pace, slamming into me over and over.

"Fuck, Quinn," his voice is gruff and breathless, "I'm gonna come."

His words barely register in my mind. I'm still on the pill, so there's no concern about that. Chase holds my ass with one hand as he slides the other between us, his skilled fingers instantly finding my clit. He plays me like a talented musician, his fingers and his dick shoving me closer to the edge.

"Oh god…" My voice trails off as the warmth begins to spread through my core and my pussy clenches around him. "I'm so fucking close."

"That's it, baby," he murmurs, diving into me deeper as he works his fingers on my clit. "Let me be your god while you come all over my cock."

My head is pressed against the bed, my eyes rolling back as I near the peak, ready for the climax. "Don't stop."

"Your cunt's so fucking wet for me right now. Such a greedy little slut." His voice is hoarse, his rhythm picking up as he thrusts into me roughly. "I can feel how close you are. Your pussy's gripping the fuck out of me."

Chase thrusts into me once more, his fingers rolling over my clit, and that's all that it takes for him to split me in two. I come apart at the seams, my orgasm tearing through my body as I lose myself around him. His head tips back, his hands gripping my ass as he calls out my name. His warmth fills me as his thrusts slow and he empties himself inside me.

My hand falls away from him and I'm in a state of pure ecstasy. Chase slowly lowers the bottom half of my body back onto the bed, putting his t-shirt underneath me to catch the mess as he pulls out. He trails his lips up my neck, traveling along my jaw until he stops at my lips.

His mouth is soft against mine as he plants a gentle kiss against my lips. As he pulls away, his blue eyes meet mine. "I don't know where the fuck you came from, but I think I want to keep you forever."

CHAPTER NINE
HAYES

The door is unlocked when I get home and I quietly slip inside as I let myself in through the front door. Soft sounds from the TV play in the distance in the living room, but I don't hear Chase or Quinn. Hell, I don't even know if she's still here, but I'm hopeful she is.

I kick my shoes off and leave my things by the front door before heading farther into our apartment. As I round the corner into the living room, that's when I see the two of them. Neither of them sees me at first and I take the opportunity to watch as their naked bodies move together.

My cock is instantly hard. Chase rocks into Quinn once more. Her face screws up, moaning loudly as he lets out a low groan. I grab myself through my pants, adjusting my erection as it strains against my clothing. I watch as Chase slowly pulls out of Quinn, his lips trailing up her torso until he reaches her lips.

I'm not jealous seeing the two of them together. If anything, I love it and want to be a part of it. I don't know where any of this is going—if it's even going anywhere—but if it continues, we'll all get our fill of one another, together or apart.

I just wish I would have walked in sooner so I could have watched them for a little longer.

I ease my way into the room, Quinn's head falling to the side as she turns to look at me. A gasp escapes her and Chase lifts his head with a smirk forming on his lips. He rolls off her, landing on his side next to her on the couch.

"I thought you weren't coming home until later," Chase taunts as he trails his fingertips across Quinn's torso. "You just couldn't stay away, could you?"

My cock throbs as I unbutton my jeans and slide the zipper down, stopping as I reach the couch. "And miss out on this? Fuck that."

Quinn's eyes are on me as I lower myself down onto my knees by the couch, spreading her thick thighs apart as I settle in between them. "What are you doing?" she questions me, the curiosity heavy in her hoarse voice.

"You'll see." I wink at her, before dropping my gaze down to her glistening pussy. Chase's cum drips from her and I slowly lick my lips, desperate to taste the two of them mixed together.

Chase is still lying beside Quinn on the couch, his hand diving into my hair as my face dips closer to the center of her legs. I run my tongue along her cunt, the sweet taste of her cum mixing with the saltiness of Chase's in my mouth. I groan, wrapping my arms around her thighs as I move her closer to the edge of the couch.

My fingertips dig into her flesh as I move one arm from her and slide my hand up Chase's leg. As I reach his cock, I feel how hard he is already and wrap my fingers around the shaft. I slowly stroke him, feeling my own erection throbbing against the side of the couch as I run my tongue through Quinn's and Chase's cum again.

Quinn moans loudly as I shove my tongue inside her, swirling it, tasting and teasing her. I pull my tongue out, swallowing both of them before suctioning my lips to her pussy. I suck Chase's cum from her, drawing it into my mouth as it mixes with hers on my tongue.

I thought I'd tasted heaven before, but I was wrong. This is it. The two of them together.

"Fucking hell," Chase groans, his words breathless as his grip tightens in my hair. "Suck my cum from her pussy."

I tug harder on Chase's cock, twisting my fist as I stroke his length over and over. Quinn's hips buck against my face as I swirl my tongue inside her again, lapping at her pussy, drinking both of them.

"So fucking good," Chase murmurs as he releases my hair and strokes the side of my face. He wraps his hand around my wrist and pulls me away from his cock. I pull away from Quinn as Chase climbs over us and heads toward his bedroom, leaving all of our clothes scattered on the living room floor.

Quinn and I get up at the same time, falling into step as we hurry after him, urgency in our strides. As we reach the bedroom door, we both pause at the threshold, our eyes finding Chase on the bed. He's on his back, his legs spread as he strokes his cock with his own hand, a smirk playing on his lips.

His eyes find mine first. "Be a good boy and come sit on my cock."

My tongue darts out, licking my lips as I step into the bedroom. It's not even a question. All he has to do is tell me what he wants and it's an involuntary submission. It's been a while since either of us have done this. I climb onto the bed and inch closer to him on my hands and knees. I stop as I reach his abdomen, taking his cock in my hand as I push his away. He lets out a harsh breath as I wrap my lips around the head and inhale him in one fluid movement. Chase grabs my thighs, pulling me closer to him until my ass is facing him.

He slides his fingers into his mouth, wetting them, as Quinn climbs onto the bed. She sits down at the edge of the mattress, her eyes fixed on us and a fire burning in her gaze. I hear the pop of Chase's lips as his fingers leave his mouth and he slides them along my crack. He pauses for one second before pressing the tip of one against my hole.

I swallow his cock again, letting it hit the back of my throat as he slips a finger into my ass, stretching me open. He pumps his hand a few times, getting me ready before he inserts a second finger. My hand slides down, massaging his balls as my head continues to bob up and down his shaft. He fucks me with his fingers for a minute, making sure that I'm ready for him before he pulls out of my ass and pushes my head away from him.

"Sit on my cock, but face the other way," he demands before spitting in his hand. I watch as he wraps it around his erection, stroking it a few times to make sure that it's wet enough before he motions for me.

I crawl across the bed, rising to my feet as I reach his thighs. Turning away from him, I face Quinn as I squat down, my back facing him. The tip of his cock is warm against my ass and I inhale sharply as I lower myself onto him. He fills me to the brim, impaling me in one thrust. His one hand finds my hip and the other finds my throat as he pulls me back against him.

My back is against his chest, my head resting beside his as I lay backward on him. His fingers are light on my skin, his touch featherlight as he keeps his hand around my throat and asserts his dominance.

"Fuck, you're so good," he murmurs in my ear as he nips at my cartilage. I feel him shift slightly as he lifts his head to look at Quinn. "Climb on top of him, baby. I want you to face us and ride his cock while he rides mine."

Quinn's gaze is heated as it meets mine. She moves closer to me, her eyes not leaving me. "You want me to fuck you?" she asks, her voice thick with lust.

"I know your pussy is soaking wet and ready for me, isn't it, Doc?"

She stands on the bed, climbing over me as she straddles my lap. Chase grabs my cock, holding it upright as Quinn slowly lowers herself onto it. She takes my entire length in one stroke, her pussy still wet from Chase's cum and from when I was licking her. She places her palms on my chest, her thighs on either side of my body and her feet on the bed beside Chase.

I plant my feet on the bed on either side of Chase's thighs and move my hips, his cock sliding out of my ass slightly. Chase's hands are instantly on my hips, holding me in place as he tops me from the bottom. I'm sandwiched between the two of them. Quinn rocks her hips, lifting herself up and down as she rides me.

Chase moves his hips, thrusting up from the bed as he holds me in place and fucks my ass. I'm a panting, fucking mess as I reach in between us, my fingers finding her clit. I play with her pussy, my chest constricting as Chase continues to fill me to the fucking brim. He drags his tongue along the side of my neck, licking and biting my skin.

The room is filled with our sounds—the moaning and groaning, the sound of skin on skin. Quinn's pussy is so wet as she clenches around my cock and Chase is so fucking hard, fucking my ass with no remorse. My balls constrict, tightening against my body as I fight the inevitable volcano building inside me that threatens to erupt at any given moment.

"It's been too long since I've fucked this ass," Chase murmurs in my ear, his fingertips digging into my hips as he continues to thrust into me. "I want you to fill her with your cum while I fill you with mine."

My teeth grit, my face contorts and my eyelids slam shut as I move my fingers against Quinn's clit. My other hand grips her ass as she bounces on my cock, rocking her hips faster. She moans loudly, my name falling from her lips as she loses herself on me.

"Come all over his cock," Chase growls at her as he pounds harder into my ass. His mouth is back at my ear, his breath warm and ragged. "Come with me, Hayes."

All it takes is those four simple words and I'm filling Quinn with my cum as Chase thrusts into my ass, one last time, losing himself inside me. My face screws up and stars immediately flood my vision. My name leaves his lips in a rush and Quinn collapses against my chest as she shatters around me. I'm on another fucking planet, consumed by both of them and the pleasure that rocks my body. We're all riding our own high, one that we created together.

At some point while we're all drifting through the abyss, Quinn slowly climbs off me, flopping down onto the bed beside Chase. I slowly climb off him, feeling his absence instantly as his cock slides out of my ass. It's a weird sensation, feeling so full even though he's no longer inside me. Chase watches both of us collapsing against the mattress with an amused expression and a smirk.

He slowly climbs off the bed and wraps each of his hands around one of my ankles and one of Quinn's, attempting to pull us along with him. Quinn rolls onto her back, giggling as she pulls her leg away from him. "Come on, you dirt balls. We all need to get showered after that."

I slowly sit up, raising an eyebrow at Chase. "You only wanna get clean so we can do this all over again."

Chase winks and Quinn laughs and sashays past him, swatting at his shoulder while heading for the bathroom. "Come along and find out."

CHAPTER TEN
QUINN

I slowly roll onto my side, feeling the bed shift before the covers are pulled back up over my shoulder. My eyelids lift and I instantly squint against the harsh light that shines through the windows behind me. It takes a moment for my brain to register where I am and what the hell happened last night.

"Good morning, Doc," Hayes's sleepy voice fills my ears. It's gravelly and sends a shiver down my spine. Something about the way he sounds in the morning makes my body instantly feel warm.

"Good morning," I say, my voice thick with sleep. I blink a few times, my eyes adjusting to the light as I see him standing off to the side. Chase lingers behind him in the doorway. His gaze meets mine and he winks before disappearing from the bedroom.

Hayes stares at me for a moment. "You like a lot of cream with your coffee, if I remember correctly."

"I do."

"How do you like your eggs?"

My eyebrows momentarily tug together. "However you'd like to make them, I suppose."

Hayes lets out a soft chuckle. "Chase is the one who cooks here, not me. He'll make them however you'd like."

"Tell him to surprise me then," I tell him with a smile as I slowly start to move into a sitting position.

"Don't get up," Hayes quickly says, causing me to stop halfway. "Let us bring you breakfast in bed. Let us take care of you, Quinn."

"You already did last night," I retort, a smirk pulling across my lips. "More than once…"

He clicks his tongue. "That doesn't count. Today is a new day." Hayes waits until I get settled back under the covers before he comes over and presses his lips against my forehead. "We'll be back with your breakfast then."

"Okay." The word gets stuck in my throat and comes out as a whisper. I watch him leave the room, feeling emotion washing over me. It's unexpected and I'm thankful that Hayes and Chase are both out of the room.

Rolling over onto my other side, I turn my back to

the door as I settle against the pillows and stare out at the snow-covered hills in the distance. In the past few days, they have made me feel things I've never felt before. They have been so attentive and so caring with me.

Every experience with them has been enjoyable. It's been better than anything I've experienced with anyone else. The sex has been absolutely mind-blowing and amazing, but it's been so much more than that.

Luke never really seemed to care about my feelings. He never made sure I was good and was always concerned with his own pleasure whenever we had sex. It wasn't often, but as long as he came, that was all that mattered. Chase and Hayes were so concerned with making sure I had an orgasm, and that it was a quality orgasm.

They didn't fall short when delivering on the quality at all.

Neither of them made me feel like I had to stay, but they both made it clear they weren't ready for me to leave yet. And if I'm being honest, I didn't want to go either.

There's a comfortableness to being around them. I've never felt more at ease. It's so difficult to explain, but it just feels right. It just feels safe and like I'm where I'm supposed to be. I've known Hayes long enough that it's not weird and I think that's why it just feels like this is how it's supposed to be with Chase.

When I ran into them on Christmas, I wasn't sure where things would go between us. By the time we ended up leaving the bar, I had a very good idea. And then after we got back here and things started to get heated, it was clear the three of us were going to end up sleeping together.

I didn't mean to fall asleep here that night; I didn't mean to stay last night. It was supposed to be a quick hookup, something to make me feel better after Luke shoved that dagger through my ego.

Yet, here I am, lying in Chase's bed while he and Hayes fix breakfast to serve me in bed.

What the hell am I doing?

This wasn't supposed to go any further than Christmas night. I shouldn't be questioning what happens next, but I am. I test-drove both cars and my god, I want to be able to drive both of them whenever I want to now.

I let my eyelids fall shut as I push the thoughts from my mind. I can't be worrying about what happens next when I haven't even talked to either of them. My thoughts are so clouded by both men and I'm certainly not supposed to be feeling anything toward either of them. I think I'm just delusional from the lack of sleep.

Hayes and Chase have kept me thoroughly satiated and equally exhausted. There are zero complaints from me on that front.

"Are you ready to eat?" Chase calls from the hallway before they walk into the room.

"I am," Hayes replies, though there's something lingering in his tone. As I roll over and sit up in the bed, the fire burning in his eyes tells me he's not ready to eat food.

He's looking like he's ready to eat *me*.

Chase carries the tray over to me and Hayes follows behind him with a cup of coffee and a glass of orange juice. He sets it down in my lap, while Hayes sets both drinks on the nightstand next to the bed.

"This looks and smells amazing," I tell Chase as I resist the urge to moan at the scent. My body feels famished, even though they've been making sure I've been eating well the entire time I've been at their place.

Hayes drops down onto the edge of the bed, carefully watching me as Chase comes over and flops down next to me on the mattress. I look back and forth at them, making a mental note that they didn't bring any food in for themselves.

"Where are your plates?"

"I'm not a big breakfast eater," Chase admits with a simple shrug before he tucks his arms under the pillow beneath his head.

"I'll eat after you're done," Hayes replies with a hoarseness in his tone.

Again, I'm not so sure he's talking about food.

Part of me wants to argue with them, but that rationale goes out the window as soon as I take a bite of the delicious eggs. This time, I let myself moan in approval. It tastes so good, I waste no time diving into the rest of the food they laid out on the tray for me.

"I think I could do this forever," I tell them, not fully processing the words before they tumble from my lips. A blush creeps up my neck and spreads across my cheeks from embarrassment.

I shouldn't have said the words, although it's not a lie. They've been pampering me and treating me like a queen. Food and orgasms will keep me happy forever.

"You know," Hayes starts as he lowers the top half of his body onto the bed, propping his head on his hand. "We were talking about where this might end up going."

I swallow a mouthful of food and reach for the coffee to take a sip. "What do you mean?"

"We were supposed to be your rebound," Chase says, his voice soft as he sits up on the bed. "So, is this where this ends?"

They beat me to it.

I wasn't planning on bringing any of this up today, but I'm glad they did. I'm not a fan of the unknown, so this helps to wash away any anxiety. It leaves all questions answered.

"I don't want it to be," I tell them with honesty. "These past few days have been absolutely amazing. It's made me realize a lot about what I want. It's shown me how low I had the bar before the two of you." I pause, letting out a breath. "I don't think this is a rebound, and I don't care to explore what else is out there."

"But you want to explore whatever this is with us?"

There's no hesitation from me.

I want this.

I want them.

"Yes."

"Good." Hayes smiles as he moves off the bed and inches closer to me. He grabs the tray, pulling it away from me before setting it on the dresser. "How do you feel about exploring right now?"

Chase starts to move closer to me on the bed as I

reach for the hem of my shirt and pull it over my head. "Fuck, you're beautiful."

"She is, isn't she?" Hayes asks him as he walks over to me and Chase. "So beautiful and all ours, aren't you, Doc?"

"Yes," I breathe as he lowers himself down to me, just as Chase slips his arm around my waist to move me between them. "I'm both of yours."

EPILOGUE
QUINN

Two Years Later

Rolling over in bed, I lift my eyelids, squinting against the harsh light pouring in from outside as I lift my hands above my head and stretch. My muscles relax, from head to toe, although they're already loose enough from the massage I received last night… we won't talk about what happened after bodies were naked and rubbed in oil.

There's a soft blanket of snow on the tops of the houses and there's a stillness, a quietness to it all. My movements are slow as I climb out of bed, slipping my feet into my snowflake covered slippers while wrapping my red robe around my body. It keeps me warm and I smile as I look out across the city, finding it to be a sleepy town on Christmas Day.

"I was going to bring you breakfast in bed."

His gravelly voice sends a shiver down my spine and straight to the center of my legs as I turn around to find Hayes standing in the doorway. He leans against the doorjamb with his arms lazily tucked into the front pockets of his plaid pajama pants. They hang low on his waist, revealing the cut V shape.

My eyes momentarily trail over his naked torso and chest before landing on his face. "Are you on the menu this morning?"

He clicks his tongue, shaking his head as he pushes away from the door frame. His strides are elongated and he stops right in front of me. His hands trail down my throat. "As much as I would love to spend the day buried deep inside of you, you know we can't do that."

"Should I bring her breakfast or is she coming down?" Chase calls from the bottom of the stairs. The sound of his voice echoes through the hallway before bouncing into our bedroom. A smile pulls on my lips and my body melts at the sound of him.

"Come on, doc." Hayes moves next to me, his hand finding the small of my back as he begins to push me to the door. "We're waiting for you to eat and open presents."

"Should we do presents first?"

Hayes smiles, his opposite hand resting on my stomach. "I think this may be one of our last years of getting to eat before we open presents."

"I think you're right." I smile back at him, my hand moving to cover his as he glides over the rounded bump. "Let me go to the bathroom and brush my teeth and I'll meet you in the dining room."

"We'll be waiting for you." He presses his lips to my temple before smiling down at my stomach and back at me. "I love you."

"I love you too."

I watch him as he makes his way down the stairs, disappearing as he rounds the corner. My footsteps are light as I walk across the hall to the bathroom and slip inside. After relieving myself and brushing my teeth, I pause by the full length mirror near the door.

As I undo the tie to my robe, I watch it fall away, revealing my body covered only by a bra and panties. My breasts are full and almost an entire cup size bigger than normal. Turning to the side, I run my hand over my swollen stomach, staring in wonderment at it in the mirror. I'm completely amazed by the wonders of the body and how we can grow an entire person inside of us.

After Hayes and Chase came barreling into my life two Christmases ago, I knew I couldn't let either of them go. What started off as casual fucking quickly shifted into dating and less than a year later, the three of us were living together. I quit working for the Archers, at the risk of Hayes and I getting in trouble and started working in a therapy office instead.

Honestly, the hours are better and it's much more accommodating for the way my life is about to change.

All of our lives.

Finding out I was pregnant six months ago was a complete shock to the three of us. I had my IUD removed because we knew we wanted to start a family, but we wanted it to happen organically. And trust me, it did. It also happened sooner than we thought. My doctor said it could take months, so it was a surprise that it happened after only one.

I don't know the exact moment the baby was conceived, nor do I know who the biological father is, but that doesn't matter. This baby is mine. It's Chase's. It's Hayes's. She is the product of love—the love the three of us have together.

They are both her father's and the biology behind it will never change that.

Chase and Hayes are both sitting at the table

waiting for me. There's an entire plate already made with my favorite breakfast foods, along with a cup of decaf coffee and a glass of orange juice.

"Look at the two of you. You are so fucking sweet," I croon with a smile on my face. I walk over to Chase first, tipping his head back as I kiss him. "I love you so much." Then I move to Hayes, repeating the same kiss. "I love you so much."

"We know what you like, babe," Chase tells me, smiling brightly as he motions for me to sit. "We made sure we covered every single one of your recent cravings."

My heart soars as I let his words sink in. Chase—the man who has an entire list constructed of what we need to do for the baby and the origin and meanings of all the baby names I picked out. I look at Hayes, feeling the same swelling of my heart muscle as it beats for both of them. Hayes—the man who won't let me lift a finger and insisted on painting the nursery by himself.

They have both been so attentive during this entire experience. Hell, they have been since that first night together. They make me their number one priority and I know they'll do the same for our baby.

"You are both so amazing, sometimes I feel like I don't deserve either of you," I admit, my voice catching on the emotion in my throat. I rub my hand over my stomach, thinking of her. "I just know you are going to be the best fathers she could ever want."

"But I'm going to be the best," Hayes adds in, winking at me.

Chase throws a piece of bacon at him. "Fuck you, because it's going to be me."

"I'll let you fuck me," Hayes shrugs, a devious smirk pulling on his lips as he looks to me. "I guess maybe we can spend the day buried inside of you."

My breath catches in my throat and there's a rush of warmth between my legs. "Fuck the food," I mumble as I push my chair back and stand up from the table. "That sounds like a much better plan."

"Fuck first and eat later?" Chase questions both of us, a grin pulling on his lips as he stands up and stalks toward me. "Although I could still eat…"

"Both of you." My eyes flash from Chase to Hayes, feeling the fire burning deep inside me at the thought of getting to enjoy both of them before breakfast.. "Upstairs now."

"Yes ma'am," they say in unison, both following hot on my heels as we step into the bedroom. I wait until they're in the room before I shut the door behind us. "Who wants to fuck me first?"

"It's Christmas, babe," Hayes murmurs as he walks up to me, his hands cupping the sides of my face.

Chase steps up behind me, his hands pushing my robe away from my shoulders, removing it completely before his lips find the side of my neck. "You get to choose."

One hand reaches back for him, my head falling against his shoulder as Hayes unhooks my bra and removes it from my body. His hands move around my full breasts, gentle and attentive as his mouth drops down to my nipple. "I want both of you to fuck me first. I want to feel both of you inside me together."

"You're such a fucking greedy girl," Chase groans, his teeth nipping at my ear as his hands snake around the front of my body.

Hayes pushes my underwear down as both of their fingers slide over my pussy in unison. Chase licks and nips at my neck, his thumb brushing over my clit. Hayes's lips find the other side of my neck as he pushes his fingers deep inside of me. "You're our greedy girl, aren't you?"

"Yes," I breathe, withering under both of their touches. Chase groans against my neck as Hayes pulls away. He begins to back toward the bed, stripping off his clothes before the backs of his knees hit the mattress. He moves onto the bed, motioning for me to follow.

"Say it and we'll let you come."

I don't know which one of them said it and I don't even care. I head straight for Hayes, climbing onto the bed and over him as I sink down onto his cock. He fills me to the hilt in one fluid movement. I inhale sharply at his length and girth, settling on top of him as I adjust.

"I'm yours. I am both of yours."

Hayes reaches over to the nightstand and pulls out a bottle of lube from the drawer. Chase climbs onto the mattress, settling behind me as Hayes hands it to him. He gently nudges me forward, but my stomach prohibits me from lying flat against Hayes. Chase slides one finger into my ass without warning.

He begins to pump it inside of me, adding another as he stretches me enough to fit himself inside. He removes his fingers and I suck in a sharp breath, instantly seeing stars as he presses his dick into me, filling my ass with his cock.

"And we're yours, Quinn," Chase moans as he thrusts into me.

"This Christmas until our last Christmas."

And I can't wait to spend every single one with them... especially if they keep starting out like this.

LOOKING FOR ANOTHER SPICY NOVELLA?

Flip the page for a look inside The Christmas Exchange, a SPICY MMF holiday novella…

CHAPTER 1

As the cab pulled up in front of my parents' old colonial home, I paused just inside the vehicle for a moment. They weren't expecting me until later this evening, but I ended up switching to an earlier flight and got in a few hours before my mother was supposed to pick me up from the airport. My movements were unhurried as I slowly climbed out of my seat and stepped out onto the sidewalk.

I tipped the driver as he handed me my bag and I stood on the curb, staring up at the house for a moment. Inhaling deeply, I sucked the clean, crisp mountain air into my lungs and closed my eyes. It had been almost an entire year since I had come back to my hometown. I would be lying if I said there wasn't a part of me that didn't miss this place.

Almost ten years ago I left for college in New

CHAPTER 1

York City, and I never looked back. The city was where I truly belonged, but there was something about the mountains that always called me back. I enjoyed the constant movement where I lived. Time moved in fast-forward, never slowing. Every now and then, it was nice to take a step back and breathe in the fresh air while staring up at the open skies that weren't obscured by skyscrapers.

There was a part of me that was a little anxious about being back in my hometown. It had been a few years since I last saw my best friends whom I grew up with. We had all grown apart over the years, even though we had tried to stay in contact. I wasn't sure if they would be back in town for the holiday or not, but I was hoping I'd see them at some point. At the same time, I was a little nervous about the possibility of running into them again.

So much time had passed, I was afraid so much would have changed.

Opening my eyes, I stared back at the house that loomed above me. I always swore this place was haunted when I was a kid, but as my eyes trailed over the Christmas lights hanging from the gutters, I found it hard to believe. It looked like the North Pole had thrown up all over the exterior of the house. My mother's style was always softer and delicate, but she didn't hold back when it came to Christmas.

CHAPTER 1

Grabbing my suitcase, I stepped up to the front gate and opened it before stepping into the front yard. The wheels of my suitcase moved over the concrete walkway as I dodged small clumps of snow until I reached the front steps. Hoisting it up, I walked across the front porch that wrapped around the house. My hand touched the cool metal handle of the front door and I pushed it down before letting myself in.

It was warm and welcoming inside, a stark contrast to the cold winter air outside. The smell of vanilla and cinnamon enveloped me, drawing me deeper into the house. The sound of my mother's voice as she hummed drifted down the hall and I left my suitcase in the foyer by the stairs before stepping into the kitchen. She was moving around the island when she caught sight of me.

A gasp escaped her and she jumped, lifting her hand to her chest. "Oh my goodness, Raegan! You scared me." She paused, her eyebrows scrunching before glancing at the clock on the stove. "Wait. Raegan? I'm supposed to pick you up from the airport after dinner."

I shrugged off my long wool coat and smiled brightly at my mother. "I was able to get an earlier flight and thought I would come early and surprise you."

CHAPTER 1

Her lips stretched into a grin and she rounded the island before pulling me in for a hug. "And what a pleasant surprise this is! I'm so happy you're here, dear." She pulled away, smoothing the arms of my sage green sweater. "How was your flight?"

"It wasn't terrible," I told her, watching her as she moved over to the counter to pour me a cup of coffee. Steam drifted from the top of the mug as she poured some caramel-flavored creamer into it before handing it to me. "I was able to get some work done on the flight, so it helped to pass the time."

I worked for one of the top marketing firms in the city and oversaw various projects for some of the biggest retail companies in the world. It was a time-consuming job, but lucky for me, I was driven and working my way to the top. My dating life was dismal and I didn't leave much time for other hobbies. I was basically married to my job.

"I'm glad you were able to get the time off to come visit."

I was an only child and I knew it was rough on my mother when I decided to fly from the nest. Especially when I moved so far away. We talked regularly and I tried to come visit when I could, but this past year was just so hectic I couldn't get the time off that I wanted to. I felt guilty, especially with the sadness

CHAPTER 1

in her smile as she looked at me in that moment, but such was life.

I smiled back at her. "Me too."

"Well, since you're home, why don't you take your things to your room and get settled in. I'm sure you're tired from traveling. I have to head to the market in a bit to get some things for Christmas dinner."

I tilted my head to the side. "I'm actually not that tired. Perhaps I could join you?"

Her face lit up. "I would love that."

"Perfect."

After taking my stuff up to my old bedroom, my mother and I headed into town to go to Finnegan's Market. It was a large warehouse that was set up with various stands, along with a small grocery store in the center. It was where most people in the town frequented to do any shopping, whether it was for food or other items. The only thing they didn't have was clothing, but if you were looking for small knick knacks, you could find it all there.

My mother and I parted ways as she stepped into the grocery store to do her shopping and I made my way around, checking out the different stands. I had

CHAPTER 1

brought my parents gifts back from New York, so there wasn't a need to buy anything here, but I couldn't resist looking at the handcrafted things you could find only at Finnegan's.

Mr. Murray had his usual stand set up with his sculptured wooden animals. Everything he made was from wood he cut down from the forest on his property and he hand-carved every single piece. I was looking at the resin cutting boards he had added to his inventory when I heard my name.

"Raegan Thompson!" The voice was deep as it rumbled from his chest. A voice I would have known anywhere. I spun around and saw Miles striding toward me.

He was one of my closest friends growing up. His parents and my parents were friends and we were literally inseparable. That was until we both left for college and moved away from Delmont Ridge. His sandy brown hair was a perfect mess on top of his head and his blue eyes met mine as he stopped directly in front of me.

The navy sweater he was wearing hugged his muscles and I allowed my eyes one opportunity to scan his physique, but only for a brief moment. If I allowed my eyes to linger any longer, it would only ignite the old feelings I used to have for him. Feelings I always kept to myself because he was one of my

CHAPTER 1

best friends. Being attracted to him would have never ended well—plus, he was always dating different girls.

"Well, if it isn't Miles Walker. What are you doing here?"

A smirk pulled on his lips. "Home for the holidays. My mother said yours told her you'd be back in town. I planned on hunting you down, but you just made my job easier."

A soft laugh escaped me and I shook my head at him. "How have you been? It's been far too long."

"You're telling me." He chuckled. "We really need to make it a habit to meet up more than just when we're both back home. I'm fairly certain we only live about an hour away from each other. You're still in Manhattan, right?"

I nodded. "You're in Jersey, just over the bridge?"

Miles nodded. "I will say, I'm not a fan of the city, but I'd deal with the lunatics on the road if it meant I got to see you."

"Yeah, well, we'll have to see about making that happen then, won't we?"

His eyes were unreadable for a moment as he stared down at me, deep into my hazel eyes. Given he was at least a foot taller, I always had to tip my head back to be able to meet his gaze. "What are you doing tonight?" He paused for a moment, his tongue

CHAPTER 1

darting out to wet his lips. "I mean, we are both back in town, so why wait until we're back on the East Coast to hang out?"

I mulled over his words. My mother didn't say anything about any plans. From what I knew, we didn't have anything officially planned until Christmas Day. "What did you have in mind?"

"Julian and I are meeting at The Swan around eight. Want to meet us there?"

My breath caught in my throat at the mention of his name, surprised to hear he was back for the holidays as well. Julian Foster. The third leg to our trio. The three of us were inseparable while we were growing up, until we graduated from high school. Julian had us beat in terms of moving far away from Delmont Ridge. He moved to an entirely different country and spent his days in the beautiful city of Venice.

I had gone to visit him once, three years ago… but that was a different story.

One I would never share with the world.

"Sure, I'll be there," I told him as my mother walked up to me. She stepped up to the two of us with a smile.

"Hi, Miles," she said softly, and he grinned at her as he pulled her in for a hug. "Your mother said

CHAPTER 1

you'd be coming home for Christmas, but I didn't expect to see you here."

Miles lifted his grocery bag and smiled sheepishly. "Just picking a few things up for the feast. It was nice seeing you," he said to my mother before turning to me. "I'll see you this evening."

"See you on Christmas, Miles," my mother said with a nod, and Miles winked at me before disappearing into the crowd. I was a little confused by her response to him. Why would she see him on Christmas Day?

I turned to look at my mother with a scowl. "Why are you going to see him on Christmas?"

My mother gave me a knowing look. "I thought I told you the plans for this year, Raegan. Eleanor, Laura, and I all decided we would get together with our families, like we used to before you guys all left for college. We're going to celebrate the holiday with the Walkers and the Fosters."

ALSO BY CALI MELLE

WYNCOTE WOLVES SERIES

Cross Checked Hearts

Deflected Hearts

Playing Offsides

The Faceoff

The Goalie Who Stole Christmas

Splintered Ice

Coast to Coast

Off-Ice Collision

ORCHID CITY SERIES

Meet Me in the Penalty Box

The Tides Between Us

Written in Ice

Dirty Pucking Play

The Lie of Us

ASTON ARCHERS SERIES

Make Your Move

Make Your Play

STANDALONES

Tell Me How You Hate Me

The Art of Breathing

The Christmas Exchange

The Christmas Rebound

ABOUT THE AUTHOR

Cali Melle is a USA Today Bestselling Author who writes sports romance that will pull at your heartstrings. You can always expect her stories to come fully equipped with heartthrobs and a happy ending, along with some steamy scenes.
In her free time, Cali can usually be found living in a magical, fantasy world with the newest book or fanfic she's reading or freezing at the ice rink while she watches her kid play hockey.

Printed in Great Britain
by Amazon